NO PLACE LIKE YOU

BRENDA BARRETT

"I like her very, very, very much," Rory stressed. "And when I bring her around, I don't want any of you to make her feel uncomfortable."

"You're not bringing her around," Bunny said through clenched teeth. "Didn't we agree that you would stay away from her?"

"I didn't agree to that," Rory said. "You said it. I silently listened."

"Ooh," Mercedes grinned, "He is indeed growing up, defying his mommy."

"But Rory…" Bunny protested.

"Leave the boy, Bunny," Bobby said. "When I was his age, if my parents told me to stop seeing someone, that's when I would see them. If you really want him to leave her, you should welcome her with open arms, befriend her, and become besties."

"Her mother runs Sensuous City," Bunny said through clenched teeth.

"The den of iniquity," Larry gasped, imitating, clutching his imaginary pearls.

Jeremiah and Mercedes hooted with laughter.

"Running a nightclub is running a business," Rory winced. "I don't see what the problem is."

"Oh, really now," Bunny snorted. "You know the kinds of debauchery that take place in those places."

ALSO BY BRENDA BARRETT

FULL CIRCLE
NEW BEGINNINGS
THE PREACHER AND THE PROSTITUTE
AFTER THE END
THE EMPTY HAMMOCK
THE PULL OF FREEDOM
REBOUND SERIES
THREE RIVERS SERIES
NEW SONG SERIES
BANCROFT SERIES
MAGNOLIA SISTERS SERIES
SCARLETT SERIES
WILEY BROTHERS SERIES
PRYCE SISTERS SERIES
THE JACKSONS SERIES

ABOUT THE AUTHOR

Brenda Barrett is an award-winning and bestselling author who has a passion for writing real Jamaican romances.

When she's not weaving words that transport readers to exotic locales, you can find her nurturing her green thumb in the garden or doting on her beloved cats.

With an infectious zest for life, this author brings a unique perspective to her writing that is both relatable and thought-provoking.

Don't be surprised if you find yourself lost in the pages of her latest work, as she seamlessly blends romance with some drama, mystery, and suspense, or even sci-fi, leaving readers wanting more.

You can connect with Brenda online at:
Brenalbar.com
Twitter.com/AuthorWriterBB
Facebook.com/AuthorBrendaBarrett

Prologue

After High School Graduation

"You can either come and work with me at Sensuous City or find a job somewhere else," Pearl pulled back the curtain in the room aggressively and allowed the sunlight to hit Jewel squarely in the face. "We are poor people; we don't have the luxury of lounging in bed."

Jewel covered her eyes. "What time is it?"

"Seven o'clock. June thirtieth. I just got in from work," Pearl said snarkily. "Now get up and start to hustle, or I will have to kick you out. My mother kicked me out when I was your age."

"You were pregnant with me," Jewel murmured. "Where is the gratitude that I actually graduated high school?"

"Gratitude!" Pearl yelled. "If you hadn't graduated, I would have done you serious damage. You are a bright girl, and you can go far. That's why I spent money on all those extra classes."

"And it paid off; I got accepted into all the universities I applied for," Jewel said smugly, sitting up in the bed and rubbing her eyes.

Pearl sat at the end of the bed and sighed. "I've been wracking my brain to find out how to send you to college. I came up with two options. First, I considered your good-for-nothing father."

Jewel sighed. "And what did he say?"

Darnell Webb was the definition of a deadbeat. First, he had denied she was his before she was born. Then when she came out looking exactly like him and his family, he had insisted on getting a DNA test because it could have been any of his brothers who fathered her.

Poor Pearl, she had the time of her life as a broke teenager on her own, trying to get Darnell on child support. When she was finally granted a reprieve by the court, Darnell was often in arrears on his child support payments. Her mother dragged Darnell to court for most of her childhood years.

Her mother's life was a cautionary tale for any young girl, especially her. Jewel had been determined to not end up like her.

"Mom?" She prompted Pearl, who was looking out into space, a snarl on her lips. "What did Darnell say?"

"He said you should work first and then pay for college; thousands of people do it every day."

"That sounds like the standard Darnell reply," Jewel said. "I expected it, to be honest. Didn't he just get another child with his girlfriend? He doesn't have money to spare."

"He has four taxis on the road," Pearl scoffed, "he can afford to at least contribute to your college funds. I had to threaten him with court for every spare cent he contributed to your welfare outside of what the court ordered him to pay. He could redeem himself and at least help you with college."

Jewel sighed. It could take all morning when her mother started going off about Darnell. "What's the second option?" Jewel asked, trying to speed up the conversation and avoiding the vitriol which would certainly follow.

"Your uncle Leonard," Pearl said, looking down at her hands.

"No," Jewel said, "oh no. Not him. Never him."

"I already ran it by him, and he said he would pay for your college, pay for your lodgment in Kingston, give you pocket money, and give you one of his cars that he is not using...."

"In exchange for what?" Jewel whispered. She knew the answer. There were no freebies from Leonard Crooks, her so-called uncle, her mother's benefactor.

"You pay him back," Pearl lay down on the bed and stared at the ceiling. "Because you are family, he'll give you two years after college to pay it back."

"Two years?" Jewel sighed, "I'll have to get a well-paying job."

"Or you can marry a rich man." Pearl turned and looked at her. "You are a pretty girl. If it's one thing your lousy sperm donor of a father has given you is the Webb genes. Use them."

"Why is there always something with this family?" Jewel mumbled, "you can't get a break."

"If you don't pay Leonard back in cash, you will have to pay him back in kind," Pearl said. "You know how it is with your uncle."

"He is sick," Jewel said. "And stop calling him my uncle."

"He is my stepbrother," Pearl grimaced, "and he is the reason we are not living on the streets and why I have a job. He built this lovely little place on family land and allowed me to run Sensuous City. Without him, where would you and I be?"

"For years you had to pay for it on your back," Jewel said. "He wouldn't even allow you to have a proper relationship with anyone because he is always in the background watching and controlling you. I don't want the same deal. I want to go to college but not that bad. I will work for a while and then take out student loans."

"Or you can go to college, work hard, and get a scholarship." Pearl turned to her, "if Leonard only pays for a year or two, you can pay him back quickly after two years."

Jewel nodded. "That sounds better."

"And be picky about the boys that buzz around you," Pearl said seriously, "only pay attention to the rich ones. The ones that can afford to step in when you need it. And not just any ordinary rich boy either; target one from a rich family. And don't, for God's sake, have sex with anyone unless there is a ring involved. There is no free milk; they must buy the cow."

Jewel snickered. "You are a fine one to talk."

"I am the best person to tell you this," Pearl said. "I see so many girls and women come to Sensuous City; they all have the same story, with a little variation. They all slept with some man who discarded them after they've had their fill; they either have a kid or two or three for these men who disappear as soon as they get what they want. They didn't learn to think highly of themselves; you are not them. You are my precious Jewel, and you are going to do better than I did in relationships and better than any woman in our family so far."

Jewel was nodding vigorously. She was all for that; there was not one successful relationship in her family, at least none that she knew about, the couples may stay together, but they were as toxic as it can be. "Where does love come into this?"

"Love is good but not necessary." Pearl scoffed. "Love is for people in romance novels or fairy tales. This is the real-world, Jewel; you must approach relationships like a business. You are young and beautiful, don't waste your good years on a man that isn't worth it. If you are smart about this, then you will go far, mark my words."

Chapter One

"**A**re you sure you're going to be alright?" Bunny asked anxiously for the umpteenth time.

Rory looked at his parents as they stood near the entrance of his apartment door. Since the moment they had driven up to the block of apartments where he would spend the next three years of university, his mother had turned into a mass of anxiety.

At least she had admitted that the place was nice, completely different from any accommodations they had when she attended the university.

The apartment complex he was in was more luxurious than a dormitory. He had his own tiny living room, a sofa and a study desk, a kitchenette, and a room with two single beds, which he would be joining together since he had no intention of sharing his space with anyone.

"And you have everything you need for now?" Bunny asked again.

"Yes, Mom." Rory nodded.

"I will bring your car during the Christmas term," Bunny said, "unless you want me to send it before that?"

"I'll be fine," Rory said, "I'll walk around for now. I don't mind being a regular student."

"Not in this luxury place." Bobby snorted. "A regular student would be in a dorm sharing space, getting the full college experience. You can lock yourself away in this place and pretend to be in a hotel for three years."

Rory grinned. "I will go to classes, Dad."

"You'd better," Bobby said. "Don't do any of that rich boy nonsense that Larry did in his first year of university. He quickly learned that he had to get a job if he squandered his opportunity."

Rory nodded. "I am not the partying type."

"And that's what has me worried." Bunny said, "you are so much of an introvert and shy with it. I am afraid that you won't go outside, meet new people, or be involved in the activities here."

"He has his friends from high school," Bobby pointed out. "He won't be lonely."

"They are all doing different majors and if Rory has his way, he will probably only hang with them because they are familiar. I can picture it now; he'll play ridiculous video games with Camden and Kenny and drink copious amounts of those fatty, salty, MSG-laden cup soups he bought several cases of."

Rory chuckled. He had only bought the instant noodle soups because Jeremiah said they could be a lifesaver and he should always have them on hand. His oldest brother was an alma mater at the same school.

"I will eat at the dining room here for breakfast and dinner. And I'll make an effort to make new friends," Rory said. "Is that a good compromise?"

His father nodded, satisfied. "You heard the boy, Bunny? He'll make friends and eat healthily. Let's go and leave him to his first taste of adulthood."

"But…" Bunny was torn, "we could stay a little. He is my baby boy."

"No, he is not," Bobby said, "he is a grown man who can't wait to get us out of his hair so that he can have some freedom from his clinging Mommy. As soon as we leave, he will hunt down his friends, and they will get up to things it's best we know nothing about."

Rory laughed, and he got up and stretched. "Mom, everything will be okay, I promise; if not, I will call you."

"You promise?" Bunny asked.

"Promise."

Rory endured an extra-long hug from her and then a brief one from his father. He opened the door and watched them as they walked away. A little scared part of him wanted to go with them.

He would never admit this out loud, but he had found the prospect of living alone daunting. He had never been on his own before. How on earth would he take care of himself without Bunny to run every aspect of his life?

"Hey, Momma's boy," he heard a shout across the hallway. He still stood at his doorway long after his parents had disappeared. They had probably left the building by now.

"Come check out my crib."

Six doors down, standing with a grin on his face, was Camden Byfield. His best friend from high school. They had both chosen this apartment complex together. He had not been sure that they would have gotten the same floor.

Rory grinned in relief. "I am pretty sure it's the same as mine."

Camden strode toward him, a can of soda in his hands, "I have something you don't have."

"What's that?" Rory frowned.

"The hottest girl I have ever seen moved into the apartment next to mine." Camden widened his eyes, "I mean hot, Rory."

Rory laughed. "Oh, really now?"

"She is Meagan Good hot," Camden said, "and probably hotter."

"Oh wow," Rory snickered, "she has met up to and surpassed your standard of beauty?"

"Oh yes," Camden nodded. "I may have to camp out at her door."

"You may find several women like that during our time here." Rory shrugged, "let's go eat something; Jeremiah says I should check out the restaurant, Biscuits, first thing."

"I don't know, man," Camden said, "I don't want to leave here until she emerges from her apartment, and I can get to see her in all her dazzling glory."

Rory sighed. "I will call Kenny and see what she's up to. I can't believe you are so excited about a girl that you don't want to eat."

"When you see her, you will understand," Camden said mysteriously.

****

"This place is nice! But what did I expect? Your aunt Precious recommended it." Pearl walked around the apartment and sat down heavily on the sofa. "I could live here."

Jewel giggled. "It is nice. I love it! But I could have done just fine in the cheapest dorm."

She sat down beside Pearl on the two-seater sofa and sighed. "I will work my butt off to get a scholarship and good grades. A dollar amount is constantly ticking at the back of my mind, climbing in the millions."

"Just concentrate on doing well," Pearl said, "work hard and enjoy your university life; your Aunt Precious is paying for your lodging and sending pocket money. That's one less thing to worry about."

"You never talk about her," Jewel said interestedly, "I was shocked when she offered to pay for lodging and to send me some money every month."

"I wasn't close to her," Pearl said, "Mama had six of us for different men. Precious and I were the only ones with the same father; our father was in and out of prison. He couldn't help himself; he'd always fall into the same bad company."

Jewel nodded. "I know the story."

Pearl nodded. "Before Mama married Norman Crooks she would send us to live with whichever community member could take care of us. We were that poor. Precious ended up living with a schoolteacher, Mrs. Jarrett."

"When Precious passed her exams and got into university, she rarely visited us at home. I think she outgrew us. We became too common for her, I guess. And then, when I got pregnant with you, she spazzed out.

"She gave me a cussing that I will remember to this day. She was so disappointed. She called me names, horrible names, and then she ghosted me. It was the worse time to abandon me. I could have done with some support at that time."

"I am so sorry," Jewel squeezed Pearl's hand.

Pearl squeezed hers back. "I got through it. We made it on the other side, you and I. And now you are here at university. How great it is that my only child did not turn out like me."

Jewel smiled. "So, what did aunt Precious do after graduating from university?"

"She got married to a rich older man," Pearl said. "I think they met here on campus. He was a featured presenter in one of her business classes. She left Jamaica with him a year after you were born, and that's it. That's all I know. She keeps in touch with Mama; I suspect she sends her money too. How else would Mama be able to live like a retiree?"

Jewel chuckled.

"Mama was probably the one who told her about you going to university because out of the blue, she called. I didn't recognize her voice at first. And voila, wouldn't you know it, your Aunt Precious is back in our lives. At just the right time too. This puts a dent in your payback to Leonard."

Jewel nodded. "It does. About the car…."

"Keep the car," Pearl said, "he said it was a gift as long as you are in university. He has half a dozen of them; he gave you one."

"It's a luxury car," Jewel said, "the gas is expensive. Not to mention the upkeep, what if I need a car part? I can't spend my pocket money on gas and expensive car parts. I don't want to seem ungrateful, but this is not a car for a student."

"Okay, I see your point." Pearl nodded. "That's why I say find yourself a rich benefactor like your aunt Precious did."

"Come on, Mom, be serious." Jewel sighed. "The answer to all my financial problems can't be to find a rich benefactor."

Pearl rubbed the back of her neck. "I am serious. Precious had a blueprint that I was too stupid to follow. She did well in school, went to university, and married a rich man. And now, after twenty-odd years, she is deliriously happy. While I, on the other hand, am laboring for Leonard and earning a pittance for my efforts. There is no way out for me. This is my life."

Jewel winced. Leonard had trapped Pearl, and she was slowly coming to realize it. He had helped her out when she needed it most. He had built them a cottage on his father's land and didn't charge them rent, he allowed Pearl to drive one of his older cars, and for a brief while, when she was in her early twenties, he had been her lover.

But he didn't keep lovers over thirty years old. If he liked the women, he made them the head of one of his businesses. All of his businesses were run by his discarded women. His liquor stores, bars, restaurants, hotels, and nightclubs. He was generous to a fault. He financed their households and bought them houses. If he had children with them, he paid for everything related to them. He was lord of his casual harem.

The downside for these women was that he didn't pay them nearly as much as they were worth; he assumed they should be grateful because he financed them in other ways. And he didn't take kindly to them having male friends.

The last two women who had broken it off with him had met in suspicious accidents. Jewel was convinced that he orchestrated or somehow caused the accidents.

"Cheer up," Pearl said, looking at Jewel's glum expression, "I do the dirty bits so that you don't have to, and I will sort out your car situation. I'll have someone come and pick up this one, and then we'll sort out an alternative. I'll tell Leonard that it's too much for a student."

Jewel nodded. "I hate that we are so dependent on him. What if one day you want to leave? What will happen to you then? Are you going to end up in a suspicious accident like Fiona and Joy?"

"We'll cross that bridge when we get to it," Pearl got up

and stretched. "In the meantime, I want you to live your life stress-free. Do well in school, have loads of friends, and make the most of this short time in life."

"It's easy for you to say," Jewel frowned, "I am a worrier, and I don't like to depend on Leonard Crooks for my education. He is unpredictable, to say the least. How can I be assured that he won't spontaneously decide to stop paying for me in the middle of the semester?"

"He won't do that," Pearl said reassuringly. "Once I am at Sensuous City he will keep to his end of the bargain. He is all we have right now, and he is a generous man. Just get your education and a rich man. Do like your aunt, Precious."

Pearl laughed heartily and pulled out her phone. "You'll be fine. Which reminds me, I told your granny that you will be in Kingston, and she said she would tell your cousin, Lester."

"Cousin Lester?" Jewel frowned. "Why would he care?"

"He cares." Pearl inhaled. "He is rich, and he is your father's cousin. He is the reason Darnell paid up his child support. I remember going to your grandmother to complain about Darnell. She made one phone call to Lester, and instantly it was paid with extra."

Pearl smiled. "Lester is the reason Darnell is even running those taxis. Lester Webb is the sole benefactor of the Webb clan; he is their bank."

"I haven't seen him since Great grandma Helen's eightieth birthday party, that was about five years ago."

"He looks like your grandfather Reese; they could be twins," Pearl said wistfully. "I should have hooked up with him; at least I would have an easier time of it before you were born."

"He's married." Jewel chastised Pearl. "His wife Kristine is really nice. I remember every Christmas, Grandma would send for me to get something from her yearly barrel."

"Oh yes," Pearl nodded, "I forgot about that. Don't be surprised if she does something nice for you when she hears you are up here. She is the one who always sends those bulk school supplies to the country for all the members of the family. I guess, in a roundabout way, she has a hand in your education. If either of them calls, say yes to whatever they suggest."

Pearl looked at her watch. "I have to get going."

"Do you want me to drop you at the bus stop?" Jewel asked.

"No," Pearl grinned. "I have a friend who is sending his driver to pick me up. I packed to stay overnight."

"Here in Kingston?" Jewel frowned, "which friend?"

"A very nice man." Pearl grinned.

"A very nice man that you met at Sensuous City?" Jewel asked incredulously.

"No," Pearl laughed girlishly. "I met him at Madge's wedding here in Kingston. He is a music producer."

Madge had been one of Pearl's 'girls,' who had participated in a music video that had used Sensuous City as a location. Madge had stood out to the famous DJ whose video it was. They had struck up a relationship and gotten married in six months.

It was still the talk of the town. The DJ was quite popular with the women and, until meeting Madge, had been pretty wild, but he was well and truly smitten now and vowed to renounce all other women. Everybody was watching their relationship with anticipation to see if he could stick with it.

"What's the name of your producer friend?" Jewel asked.

"Chex Hastings," Pearl smiled. "If things take off, I will introduce you to him. But then again, maybe not. I don't want the competition. You look like one of the hot girls I always see hanging around him. I don't want to be competing with my own child."

"But you are the quintessential hot girl," Jewel snorted, looking at her mother, who looked more like an older sister. Nobody would believe Pearl had a child old enough to be attending university.

She had just turned thirty-four, had an ideal hourglass shape and was slim but curvy in all the right places. She had a pert little nose, generous bow-shaped lips, and eyelashes that were so thick they looked unreal.

Pearl was pretty and outgoing, and fun. And Jewel was genuinely worried that she was getting herself into a situation that wasn't like her.

Pearl didn't date. She had been single for as long as Jewel could remember.

Apart from the clandestine relationship with Leonard, before he broke it off when she aged out of his requirements, Pearl had been living like a nun. Partly because Leonard would have a hernia if she saw anyone seriously and partly because her experiences with men and the things she saw made her super picky and anti-man.

To see her now, giggling and giddy, worried Jewel.

"You have never done anything like this." Jewel voiced her horror. "What do you know about this guy?"

Pearl pulled out her mirror to freshen her makeup and ensure that the pixie cut she had dyed blonde was still in perfect order.

"He is thirty-six, handsome, my height, built like a boxer. But you can take your mind out of the gutter Missy. I am not going to meet him to hook up. There will be a party at his place. He invited me, and I agreed to go because it coincided with dropping you off here. I'll be spending the night at Madge's place after the party."

"Oh," Jewel said.

"Who knows what can happen?" Pearl smacked her lips together. "Chex Hastings is loaded."

"But he doesn't sound stable or someone you would have a long-term relationship with," Jewel pointed out. "I thought you said you wanted marriage and children with a stable man?"

"I do." Pearl nodded, "but it doesn't hurt to put yourself out there, go to an outing or two, and meet people."

"Be careful," Jewel said worriedly.

"Yes, Mommy," Pearl grinned. "I will be. Chex is sending his bodyguard and driver to pick me up in a bulletproof car. The driver's name is Danger, so you know he doesn't fool around."

"I meant be careful with yourself," Jewel said. "You might think you are tough and have seen it all, but you can get hurt like the rest of us. You are, after all, but a mere woman. You can fall hard for a guy; you are not immune."

Pearl hugged and kissed her, smearing most of her freshly applied lip gloss on Jewel's cheek. "I don't know how I was so blessed to have such a smart, loving child, but I am blessed, and I appreciate you."

Her phone rang, and she answered. "My ride is here. Call me if you need anything. I'll come running."

She left the apartment.

Jewel opened the balcony door; she had a good view of the parking lot from her apartment. She watched as Pearl got into the car, and then she slumped on the door. She missed her already.

She was used to being alone, but somehow today felt bittersweet. She wished she had a friend to call or someone to hang out with to share this new experience, but none of her friends from high school had come to this university.

Her closest friend, Annette, went to the US on a track scholarship.

She would have to see about making new friends. And she wasn't going to do it sitting in her room. She checked the new student newsletter for the itinerary. They had a ton of things planned, but they would start tomorrow. She was free today and was feeling hungry. She could grab a meal and maybe do some exploration. There was a restaurant named Biscuits that was close to the apartment. She had driven past it when they came in. She was curious to see what they served there.

Chapter Two

"**I** thought you said you weren't coming to hang with us," Rory said to Camden. When he sauntered into Biscuits while they were in the middle of ordering.

"I know," Camden said sheepishly, "but I saw the fairy tale princess heading out, and she was walking toward here. I rapidly walked ahead of her and paused for a while; I saw that she was definitely coming in here, so that's why I am here now."

"Which fairytale is this princess from?" Audra snorted.

"Beauty and the Beast." Kenny chuckled. "With Camden being the Beast."

"He's talking about a girl that just moved into our building," Rory said. "He is acting like it's the first time he is seeing a girl."

"A girl like her, in real life," Camden said, "I mean, I got a good look at her just now, and I am even surer now than before that she is going to be the future, Mrs. Byfield."

Kenny and Audra laughed. Rory didn't because the girl in question walked into the restaurant, and everything around him seemed to freeze in time.

She was beautiful. For once in his life, Camden was not exaggerating. She had long extra thick curly hair, which she wore in a ponytail, smooth cinnamon skin, almond-shaped brown eyes, and the reddest cupid bow lips he had ever seen on a woman.

He didn't know how long he stared. He knew that Audra and Kenny had stopped grinning and were staring at her. And Camden was straining his neck to see her. Maybe the whole restaurant was staring at her.

She took it all in stride. She certainly seemed unbothered by it. She went to the cashier to order her meal, pointing at the daily special and then turning around to scan the tables to see if there was an available seat.

There was one by the door. She seemed like she was contemplating whether to sit there. He knew the exact moment that she registered that he was staring. She looked straight at him and smiled.

"Good Lord," he swallowed nervously.

"Invite her over," Camden whispered fiercely.

She turned away before Rory could act.

"You should have invited her over," Camden said, disappointment in his voice.

Rory didn't realize that he was holding his breath. He let it out with a whoosh. "I couldn't have invited her over. She wasn't looking over here long enough for me to do that."

"She is not all that," Audra said dismissively, "I doubt her hair is real, and she must have on tons of makeup for her skin to look that smooth."

"Her body is definitely enhanced." Kenny chipped in, "how did she get her waist so tiny and her butt so perky. She has the perfect shape; she couldn't have been born looking like that. No one is born like that."

"She probably did surgery," Audra said, "rich girls do a lot of things to themselves these days."

"Which is a waste of money," Kenny muttered. "But I guess it keeps your father, the plastic surgeon, quite busy, and paid."

Audra laughed. "Whoever did her work is good. Maybe it was my dad. You should ask her."

"You are not to ask her any such thing," Rory said hoarsely. "Millions of women naturally look like that."

"I don't care what she did with her hair or body. I think she is perfect," Camden said dreamily, "I can picture us now, sitting together in class playing footsie under the desk."

Audra chuckled. "She is probably dumber than a doorknob."

"Dumb people don't go to university." Rory frowned at Audra.

"They do," Audra said, "probably her rich daddy paid them to take her. Maybe he financed a library or something."

"She is definitely not on scholarship like me," Kenny snorted. "Her bag alone could feed me for the semester."

"Enough." Camden hissed as she walked past them with her tray. She had ordered stewed chicken, the daily special. "I am going to find out her name and introduce myself as soon as she sits down, I am going over."

"You were always brave," Audra said, "unlike Rory here. He would never do something like that."

Rory nodded. "True, I am a shy guy."

"Shy guy, my foot. Do you know how many girls liked you in high school, and you paid them dust?" Audra asked.

"She means that she liked you," Kenny grinned. "And you paid her dust."

"Audra has always been a good friend; I prefer us that way." Rory smiled to take the sting out of the statement.

Audra shrugged. "Whatever, you'll be sorry you missed out by not tying me down. But maybe it's for the best. I am going to find myself a fellow doctor to marry. Someone who will understand the workload. We'll be a power couple like my mom and dad."

Rory smiled. He pitied the man who would take her on. Audra had to be in charge. She had to direct activities. He was surprised she didn't order for him and Kenny just now.

She usually didn't allow them to use their power of choice around her. Especially Kenny Carter, her faithful sidekick since infant school. Kenny was even more beholden to Audra since Audra's parents sent her to university. Every year, the doctors, one a plastic surgeon and one an orthodontist, chose a student to put through university as part of their charity organization.

It went without saying that this year it would be Kenny. She was Audra's friend and very bright, especially in Information Technology.

Rory wondered what would happen if Kenny decided to ditch Audra. He could smell it coming. Audra was going to do her bachelor's degree in medicine, and Kenny was going into computer programming.

Meeting like this would become rare when school started properly; the four were in different fields.

He was going into architecture, and Camden would be doing law. The thought saddened him; he would have to make new friends, as his mother had said.

"Okay, I am going in," Camden said decisively. "She is onto her third bite. I am going to tell her that I am considering ordering the same thing and ask her if I should."

"Leave the girl in peace," Kenny said, "I ordered the daily

special. It is good. Why don't you go and order your food and pretend to hang with us."

"No thanks," Camden stood up, "you people are the past. I now walk toward my future."

Rory snickered. Audra rolled her eyes. Kenny sighed.

"Why did I think college would change things between me and him?" Kenny asked forlornly.

"He's young; let him date around," Audra said, "how many college sweetheart relationships do you see lasting?"

"Quite a few," Kenny said wistfully. "Before my dad died, he and my mom were high school sweethearts."

"Aw," Audra said sympathetically, "you'll have to do like me and face the reality that people like Camden and Rory will probably get married and start families at fifty. That's how long it will take them to mature."

Rory chuckled. "I could do marriage before that."

He glanced behind to see what Camden was up to, and his eyes connected with the girl. It was quite unexpected. Rory held her gaze and tried to force himself to act normally, but he couldn't. There was something about her that was pulling him in. His heart rate accelerated; his mouth became dry.

He had never felt so hopelessly drawn to someone in all his life.

She was staring at him, too. The tension between them was palpable.

He dragged his eyes from hers. He wasn't here for romance and crushes. Besides, Camden saw her first and was actively pursuing her. He would meet other girls, and there would be other moments.

****

Except there weren't any other girls like her. And Rory

wasn't immune to her, not by a long shot. He found himself drawing her face in his sketchbook a million times. He discovered all sorts of things about her as September melted into October. She was in the same classes as Kenny because they were doing the same major. She was laser-focused on her work and freakishly brilliant. At least, that was what Kenny said.

As for Camden, she rebuffed all of his advances, she was friendly but distant with him, and he had finally moved on. Rory rarely saw her those first couple of weeks, though they lived on the same floor. And he longed to see her, even if it was from afar.

"So, there is a party tomorrow night...." Camden said. They were sitting in Rory's apartment, drinking cup soup and playing Minecraft. Their current game was a multiplayer world they had set up almost two years ago.

It was Friday night, and the weekend was shaping up to be the same old.

"I was planning to go home tomorrow." Rory looked up from his game. "I want to take some measurements to begin drawing my house."

"Ah, your house. The Nelson family coming of age gift." Camden nodded, "why don't you ask Jeremiah to do it?"

"No," Rory said, "I have to do everything myself. No one is to interfere. Those are Bobby Nelson's rules. Besides, I have to prove to him that my mother has not sissified me. I spent much time with my mom versus him when I was growing up. He has hinted that he thinks I know more about hairstyles and shoes than houses."

"You can be a bit of a momma's boy. That could become a problem for your relationships."

"No, it won't," Rory said emphatically, "she has two other boys; they have had relationships, and she does not interfere."

"She has a different relationship with them," Camden pointed out, "you are the one she has turned into her little girlfriend. Why doesn't she have the same relationship with her only girl? I will never know."

Rory sighed. "My mother and I share a love for art and music; we have a lot of things in common. Mom and Mercedes do not have the same tastes."

"I see." Camden placed the laptop on the chair before him. "Did Mercedes have to build her own house too?"

"Yes." Rory nodded, "and she did it while in college. She started in her third year, though."

"Come on, your father must have helped," Camden had always been fascinated with his family's coming-of-age tradition of handing over an empty property to all of the children when they turned eighteen. "What does she know about construction?"

"Everything." Rory chuckled. "She had to work in the business just like us. Dad didn't have her doing the rough stuff like mixing mortar, but she has done it before. She can do the grunt work and the more sophisticated bits like reading a plan. And when she was doing her house, she was the one that supervised it. Larry and Jeremiah probably asked for more advice than she did."

"She is hot." Camden grinned. "I can't imagine concentrating on a site if she is my boss."

"Do you imagine her wearing dresses and heels?" Rory laughed, "And stop lusting after my sister. I don't like it."

"But I would make a fantastic brother-in-law," Camden said, "I am already your friend. There would be no need to adjust to a new man in your family commune."

"So, I guess you are over Jewel now?" Rory asked, waiting for the answer with bated breath.

"Yes," Camden smirked, "Jewel Webb is a computer. A beautiful, wonderful machine. I don't think she is human. She is probably only programmed to smile and wave."

Rory grinned. "Oh really? Did you tell her that?"

"I have not gotten the chance to tell her anything. She is all about schoolwork and classes; who is so focused in the first year?" Camden scowled, "she is causing me to move on."

"Good," Rory grinned.

"It's not as if you will have a chance with her either," Camden smirked. "I think she is into older men."

"She is?" Rory asked, a deflated feeling gripping him.

"Oh yes," Camden nodded, "I saw her heading into a car this evening with a man who could be her father. She was happy to see him and kissed him on his cheek. It's the most animated I have seen her in a while."

Rory swallowed. "Maybe it was her father."

"One would hope," Camden snickered, "but somehow, I doubt it."

Rory grimaced. He didn't want to hear any more. He closed his computer lid. All of a sudden, he had lost the drive to play. A part of him felt deflated.

"About that party," Camden said, closing his computer lid as well. "It's one of my dad's old friends and client. The client hired a name-brand architect to do the house and will be doing the unveiling of his mansion in the hills. I thought that would be something you would appreciate."

"Is it Ray Conrad?" Rory looked at Camden incredulously.

"Yeah, I guess that was his name. He had two first names." Camden shrugged, "I told my dad I would give it a hard pass, but he said I should come along and be exposed to the movers and shakers of this country. I told him I would invite you along since that sounds like more your speed."

"Yes," Rory nodded, "I am interested. Why didn't you lead with that? I love his designs. He's an award-winning architect, a master among his peers. It would be an honor to go to an unveiling of one of his houses."

"Well then," Camden picked up his computer again, "sounds like the snooze fest of a party will be quite up to your speed. My dad will be picking us up at seven. Be ready."

Chapter Three

Two months into university life and Jewel was happily settling in. Her Introduction to Programming teacher had the class design an app in real-time. She was so engrossed in learning new concepts that it didn't feel like school.

That class, especially, had exceeded her expectations about what her time at university would be like. She was doing real-world things in her courses, and it was shaping up to be quite the experience.

She had made friends with various people in her different class groups, and her weekends were busy.

She canceled all her plans for the weekend, though, when her cousin Lester called.

"Jewel," Lester said, "so sorry I was not around when you arrived at the university. Kristine and I just got back from Canada. Congrats on this milestone!"

"Thank you, Lester," Jewel said.

"How are you settling in?" Lester asked.

"Great," Jewel replied, her voice muffled. She had been getting ready for a Friday morning class, and she was trying to put on a shirt and talk at the same time.

"Are you busy this weekend?" Lester asked, "we recently built a house, and I am throwing a party. You are invited to stay for the weekend. Kristine says she will take you shopping, so you don't have to worry about what to wear."

"Oh wow," Jewel whistled. "Thank you."

Lester laughed. "It's nothing. You probably don't know this, but your grandmother was kind to me when I was younger. She had six boys of her own, and she treated me like one of her own. There was a time I lived with her after my mother left for England. Your father was still a baby then. I grew up thinking of him as my baby brother. I haven't quite managed to shake that feeling, though Darnell makes it hard to keep those warm, brotherly feelings sometimes."

Jewel chuckled. "I understand exactly what you mean."

"Is seven o'clock good for you? I'll pick you up," Lester asked.

"Yes," Jewel said. "It will be fine."

She went through the day wishing she could call her grandmother to get more details on Lester because she was sorely lacking in family history. However, cell phone service was still spotty in the section of Cascade Hills where her grandmother lived. Being up there was largely living off the grid. People still went up there to camp and escape it all. There was a nature preserve at the top of the hill, near where her grandmother lived, which was marketed as a place to get away from it all. That was how remote a location it was.

There was a time when she used to spend her summers with her grandparents. She would join her cousins on the wraparound veranda and listen to the stories that her grandfather, Reese Webb, would tell. Most of the stories were about Jamaican myths and legends. Like the mermaid at the bottom of the river at Cascade Hill Bridge or his many encounters with a creature called a rolling calf. Those kinds of things were exciting, Jewel remembered.

She used to fall asleep when he started talking about family, though. She wished she had listened. If she had known that she wouldn't have her grandfather around, maybe she would have paid more apt attention, Jewel thought to herself.

When she was ten, he contracted pneumonia. He died two weeks after his twin brother, Reid, who also died from a respiratory illness.

Lester was waiting for her in her apartment parking lot at exactly seven. "It's so good to see you," Jewel said.

Lester Webb looked like a young version of her grandfather. Why hadn't she taken note of that before?

"I haven't seen you since great grandma's birthday party a couple years ago," Jewel smiled.

"I know," Lester nodded. "I can't believe how big you've gotten. One minute you are a wee thing, and the next, you are a beautiful young lady, all grown up. You look so much like my sister Octavia. It's staggering how the genetic lottery can play out. But then again, why should I be surprised; your grandfather and my father were identical twins. Technically, your father and I are genetic brothers and not just cousins. Added to that, our mothers are sisters."

"Who is Octavia?" Jewel asked, getting in the car.

"My older sister by two years," Lester explained. "She died tragically in an accident which also took her ex-husband's life. They couldn't have children, and she was obsessed with it. That was partly what caused problems in her marriage, and I think it made her a little mad."

"If she were alive now and saw you, she would spoil you rotten," Lester said.

"Oh wow, that explains why I have never heard of her," Jewel whispered, "I am so sorry to hear that she is no longer around."

"It was long ago, but it still stings," Lester said. "In part, she is why I renovated this house I am throwing the party at. Her husband, Henry Monroe, had given it to her in their divorce. I inherited it when she died."

"I left it alone for years, and then someone pointed out that the area had undergone some development; when I checked it two years ago, it had really come into its own. What was once a forgotten rural township is now one of the hottest areas outside Kingston. I thought I should put something up that takes advantage of the views. Kristine loves it. She is already calling it our retirement house," Lester said.

"Sounds nice," Jewel said. "I can't remember meeting Kristine."

"She spends six to eight months in Canada," Lester said. "That's where our kids are based. Our daughter Krista recently had a baby. Kristine just popped in for the housewarming. She will fly out in three weeks, and she's enjoying being a grandmother. As for my son, Kristof, he is on tour with his band. He can't make it to the housewarming, but that's okay."

"Is it a popular band?" Jewel asked, interested. "It would be exciting to have a cousin in a popular band."

"Nope." Lester sighed. "They are not even that good, but they take it seriously, and it keeps him busy and sober. Sometimes, I wish I had a relationship with Jeremiah. He has my work ethic, went to university, works hard, and is developing a reputation in his chosen field. He is the only child doing something with his life, a child to be proud of."

"And who is Jeremiah?" Jewel asked.

"He is the child I had out of wedlock," Lester shrugged.

"There was a time when I stepped out of the relationship with Kristine, and I fell in love with Bonita. When I found out that she was pregnant. I panicked; I didn't want Kristine to find out. I was foolish enough not to claim Jeremiah. In fact, I urged Bonita to have an abortion. Thankfully she didn't; she got married before Jeremiah was born, and her husband officially adopted him. But I have always kept tabs on him."

Jewel nodded. "Does he know you are his biological father?"

"Oh yes," Lester sighed. "My parents found out about the whole thing and kept in touch with him. He wouldn't know about me if it were up to his mother. She hates my guts. I really did that woman badly. I didn't mean to; I genuinely loved her and fell like a ton of bricks. I sometimes wonder, if I had left Kristine and chosen her, what would my life look like? I don't actively dwell on it, but I sometimes think about it."

"Never make my mistake Jewel," Lester said.

Jewel looked at him. "My mother thinks otherwise," she said. "She says I should marry for money and let love be damned."

"No," Lester said. "Take it from me, if you find someone to love, and they love you back, it's a blessing. If they are not rich, then work together to achieve your goals. Strive to be with someone who is ambitious and willing to work with you. The rest of it will work itself out."

Jewel smiled. "That sounds like more balanced advice than what Pearl constantly harps on about."

"Lester nodded. "Take it from me, I married for money. At this point in our lives, Kristine and I are just good friends; we live separate lives. She spends most of the year in Canada. I run the company that her father left behind. We will never divorce; we have too many legal and familial ties, and none of us are up for that unraveling. I have my girlfriends; they know I'll never leave my wife. As for Kristine, she is content with her grandchildren."

"What a sad life," Jewel said softly.

"I guess it would seem that way," Lester admitted. "I try not to dwell on it. But on to more positive things," he turned onto a road marked Irish town. "How is university life so far? Tell me everything."

****

The house was gorgeous. Their approach to it through the winding driveway flanked by cypress trees had not prepared her for its unique beauty. It was a two story structure that was a combination of modern and rustic styles. It had stone accents and windows everywhere, no doubt, to take advantage of the surrounding views.

Kristine met them at the door, and she greeted Jewel with enthusiasm. "I am so happy to meet you! Come on in, come on in! I hope you packed light because we are going shopping!"

After a quick tour through the house, with one room more breathtaking than the rest, she was shown to her bedroom, which had a fireplace and a spectacular view of the mountains outside. Kristine's idea of going shopping involved calling a personal shopper who spoke to Jewel at length about her dress and shoe size, color preferences, and activities.

After a sumptuous dinner with Kristine and Lester on Friday night, she retired early to sleep. There was something about the mountain air that made her especially sleepy. She could barely keep her eyes open through dinner.

When she woke up, the house was already abuzz with

activity. Several people were flitting about preparing the place for the party.

"Ah, sleeping beauty is awake," Kristine said, smiling at her when she arrived in the kitchen. She had been talking to a lady dressed in a suit that looked tailored just for her.

"This is Heather from last night," Kristine said. "She arrived with your wardrobe. Do you want to eat first or go sifting through the clothes?"

"The clothes," Jewel said. "I still feel full from last night's dinner."

Heather had excellent taste in clothes.

When Jewel finished trying on pieces and mixing and matching, she had a complete wardrobe.

She couldn't wait to tell Pearl about this experience. Her mother would flip out from the decadence of it. Even she was flipping out a little. She had no idea people lived this way. When she wanted clothes, she saved up her money and went to a store, or she got pieces from a generous family member, and those were usually a hit or miss.

She had never gotten all new clothes like this before. Kristine had even brought new suitcases for her to put them in.

"Thank you so much, Kristine," Jewel gushed when Heather had left and she was sitting among a pile of new designer clothes.

Kristine smiled. "It's no problem. It gives me great pleasure to do this. I want you to have a good time tonight. Wear the red dress."

Chapter Four

Rory was impressed as he looked at the luxurious mountain home that was designed by his architectural design hero, Ray Conrad.

"It's beautiful," he said, snapping a picture of the exterior of the place.

"We will get a personal tour from the man himself," Camden's father, Jim Byfield, gushed with barely held glee.

"It's just a house," Camden said, completely unimpressed. "Are any girls going to be at this party?"

"You are so predictable," Jim growled.

Rory snickered. Camden and his father had the same conversation in different variations almost daily.

Ray Conrad and the homeowner appeared at the entrance, preventing them from continuing with their bickering.

"Hello, Lester," Jim said jovially, "Sorry to show up with a crowd. My plus one is my son, who decided to carry a plus one. I couldn't say no. Apparently, Rory is a fan of yours,

Ray."

"Rory Nelson?" Lester raised an eyebrow and shook his hand. "Small world."

Rory was puzzled. Where did this man know him from?

"Your mother is Bonita Nelson," Lester said matter-of-factly. "You look a lot like her."

"So I've been told," Rory said.

Lester grinned. "You don't know who I am, do you?"

"Well, no," Rory said.

Lester laughed. "The name is Lester Webb. I am sure that your mother might have mentioned me in a not-very-flattering light. She was a very close friend of mine while she was at university."

"Oh," Rory nodded, "I have heard your name before, of course."

"We should talk some more tonight." Lester chuckled. "You are always welcome here, Rory Nelson. As a matter of fact," he turned to Camden, "you boys will probably know my cousin, Jewel. She just started university. She is here too."

"Jewel Webb is your cousin?" Camden asked incredulously.

"I see you know her," Lester said. "She is upstairs getting ready. You will see her shortly. Let's proceed with the tour before the others get here. They will get a virtual tour by the poolside where the party will be held. Jim here is an exception. We go way back to Cascade Hill days."

Jim nodded. "We were classmates and played on the same cricket team."

Rory could barely concentrate after discovering that Jewel was here in this house. He didn't know what had him more in shock, that Lester was 'the' Lester Webb, his mother's ex and his brother Jeremiah's biological father, or that Jewel, his secret crush, was Lester's relative.

His mother would be very displeased if she heard that he was touring Lester's house. As far as she was concerned, Lester was the devil incarnate. Throughout the years, she did not speak fondly of him whenever his name was mentioned.

There was a story about him trying to kill her. That was how his mother had met his father, Bobby Nelson. Bunny had been trying to escape Lester after telling him she was pregnant with his baby. He had apparently "spazzed out" and would have killed her to cover up his transgressions from his wife. Bunny had run down the hallway and into a group of men renovating the apartment, and Bobby had been one of the men.

He had saved her from Lester, taking her out of his vicinity. According to Bunny, Bobby had saved her life and married her a couple of months later while she was pregnant with Jeremiah.

Rory had heard the story so many times. It was his parents' origin story. He had always imagined Lester to be more ruthless looking.

He didn't seem like a potential killer. Maybe his mother had been mistaken.

Rory sneaked glances at him while they toured the house. Lester was normal, engaging, and friendly. But what did a killer look like anyway?

Even Camden was taken in by him. They eventually ended up at the poolside. It was an infinity pool that was lit up to look like a swath of electric blue.

The DJ was already playing music, and people were trickling in.

Rory had many questions for Ray Conrad, who seemed quite flattered that he had a young architecture student interested in his work.

Camden wandered off. He was bored with their

conversation.

Admittedly, Ray had a way of speaking that took a bit of getting used to; his sentences contained long pauses as if he were searching for words.

"Oh my Gosh," Ray whispered. "Lady in red."

"I like the song too," Rory said.

Ray wasn't listening to him; he was staring slack-jawed straight ahead.

Rory knew without turning around that it was Jewel behind him. She seemed to generate that kind of response from men.

He spun around, and there she was. Her arm was linked to Lester's, who was escorting her along the way like a proud father. He was stopped several times by different people as he introduced her.

When he reached them, Rory swallowed nervously. Jewel looked expensive, pretty, and sophisticated beyond belief in a red dress that seemed to flow around her as she walked.

As if on cue, the DJ started playing the song lady in red when he saw her.

"Now this is my cousin, though technically her father is genetically my brother because our fathers were identical twins and indistinguishable from each other," Lester said proudly. "I always tell people my family members are beautiful. Maybe now you lot will believe me."

Jewel giggled.

"Jewel, this is Ray Conrad. He designed the house, and Rory Nelson goes to your school."

Ray was nodding like a marionette. He could barely form a sentence as he stammered. "Nice to meet you."

Rory, on the other hand, was acting composed.

"I have seen you around school. In fact, we live on the same floor," Rory said.

Jewel smiled. "I know. I have seen you around, too," she replied.

She had? Rory's heart picked up speed.

Lester swept her away to introduce her to some of his other friends before he could find some witty response. Rory excused himself from Ray, who had lost all interest in their conversation; he appeared dazed and star-struck.

He headed to the other end of the pool, where several food stations were strategically placed. There was quite a spread. He found a table nobody had occupied yet and sat down to dig in.

Camden was occupied with a guy who was demonstrating how to fly a drone at night. He liked being at the fringes of the party, watching people around him chatting with each other. Of course, his eyes kept straying to Jewel in her red dress that hugged all her curves lovingly.

She was way out of his reach. She was the type of girl that you looked at from afar. She was that girl you knew you wouldn't get a chance with, but it didn't stop you from having fantasies.

And even if they were to end up together by some stroke of luck, how would that work? She was Lester Webb's cousin. How would he hide that little bit of information from his mother? And could he even hide it? Jewel looked a lot like Lester if you observed them from afar.

He imagined his mother would not be too pleased with his choice of partners. It would probably cause a mini-quake in his house.

"So here you are," Jewel said, pulling out the chair opposite him and placing her plate on the table. "I was looking all over for you."

"You were?" Rory asked. He wished his voice hadn't gone squeaky.

He inhaled deeply; he could smell her perfume. It was so light and pretty that he could sniff it all night.

"Ah yes," Jewel smiled. "Excuse me if I scarf this down. I am famished. I spent all day trying on clothes and was afraid to go into the kitchen and disrupt the flow of things; everyone was busy for tonight. So I didn't get a snack."

Rory nodded. "I had no idea you were related to the Webbs from Trelawny. I am from Trelawny."

Jewel nodded. "I heard. You are friends with Kenny. She and I are in the same group for a project. She talks about you and Camden and your school days."

"I had no idea Kenny talked about us," Rory said. "Why weren't you at our school?"

Jewel laughed. "Because your school is for the rich and connected, I am neither of those things."

"You could have fooled me," Rory smiled at her indulgently. She was trying to act down-to-earth and humble. He wasn't buying it; she was related to Lester Webb. She had spoilt rich girl stamped on her face.

"I am surprised you are hanging with me; you are the belle of the ball; you had Ray Conrad stammering, and you nearly had a few of those old guys genuflecting when you walk by."

Jewel laughed. "Genuflecting, huh? I haven't heard that word in a while."

Rory shook his head. "You made the world-famous architect scramble his words."

"I thought that was the way he spoke," Jewel mused. "I struggled through a conversation with him earlier. He was talking fast, then slow, and tripping over his words. I barely heard a thing."

"How does it feel to have so much power over men?" Rory asked.

"I don't have power over men; people being tongue-tied and drooling over you is not power." Jewel scoffed. "I don't kid myself, that is. People assume so many things about you when you have a particular look. You are never admired for your intellect; you must try twice as hard to make people sit up and listen. You are constantly judged to be an airhead with no thought but fashion and makeup. Nobody is interested in getting to know the real person behind the face; there is a personality behind this face."

"Wow," Rory murmured, "In other words, I should see past your beauty and get to know the real you?"

Their eyes connected and held.

He suddenly understood what it was to be swallowed up by someone's gaze. He felt as if they were touching.

"Do you think you can manage that?" Jewel asked. "Because I would like to get to know you better."

"Yes, I can manage that," Rory said huskily.

The attraction was right there between them, and she felt it too. It was mutual. It was potent and almost frightening in its intensity.

They were going to mean a lot to each other. Nobody had to tell him that. He could feel it in his soul.

Chapter Five

"**D**elivery for Miss Jewel Webb." Thea knocked on the door for the fifth time that day.

"Just leave it at the door, Thea," Jewel called out.

"I'll get it," offered Kenny. "Someone might steal it."

Kenny opened the door, and Thea looked past him to Jewel, who was nose-deep in code and not remotely interested in yet another gift.

"Remember my tip, Jewel," Thea said, disgruntled. "None of this personal delivery is free."

Jewel dragged her eyes from the screen. "What's your fee again?"

"Two hundred per trip," Thea smirked. "You owe me a thousand now."

"I'll pay you later," Jewel said. "I'll have to go to the ATM."

"Okay," said Thea, taking one more look at the large gift basket. She paused. "Maybe you can give me something from the basket for payment instead."

"Take whatever you want," Jewel said.

Thea clapped her hands in glee, unwrapped the basket, and took out the bottle in the center.

"That's a magnum champagne," protested Kenny. "The next fifty trips up here better be free," Thea smirked. "Okay, deal."

"Girl, what did you do to these men at that party?" Kenny closed the door and looked at her in awe.

"I did nothing. I hung out with Rory for most of the night. We talked and talked. I never got a chance to interact with anyone else for any length of time. They must have asked my cousin for my address. Half of the names on the baskets, I can't remember."

Kenny snickered. "I can't believe Rory Nelson was a bigger attraction than this guy here," she read the card. "Ray Conrad."

"Oh, he's the architect that did my cousin's house," Jewel said absently. "Of course, Rory was a bigger attraction than all of them. I happen to like Rory. I've been dying for him to talk to me since I first saw him in Biscuits. He hadn't approached me, so I had to make the first move. I've never ever done that before."

"You did?" Kenny placed the gift basket among the others and sat down beside Jewel. "Tell me more."

"There's nothing to tell," Jewel shrugged. "I'm drawn to him. I can't explain it. I've never felt this way in my life. I'm still trying to process it."

"I can understand that," Kenny said. "Rory is handsome. All the little girls would hang on to his every word in prep school, not that he would say much. He's the quiet type. Audra would do cartwheels in front of him for his attention, and he wouldn't budge."

Jewel looked up from her computer. "Tell me about Rory."

"I need sustenance," Kenny got up. "What do you have in these giant baskets? This one is full of fruits and chocolates."

"These are expensive things," Kenny whistled. "I lucked out in forming a friendship with a highly sought-after rich girl with wealthy admirers."

"You are the rich girl," Jewel said. "I am not."

"I am quite far from being a rich girl," Kenny snorted. "I am here on scholarship. I'm currently wearing Audra's hand-me-downs. I'm the friend everybody pays for because they know I'm not in their income bracket."

"You went to private school," Jewel pointed out.

"Because my mother taught there and received a huge discount," Kenny shrugged. "She reasoned that, I would benefit from the small classes and individual attention at the school, especially since my grades were good. All my siblings went to public school."

"Oh," Jewel chuckled, "it seems like we're making false assumptions about each other."

"I don't know if my assumptions are false," Kenny washed the grapes and found a bowl for them. "You're related to Lester Webb, you live in the most expensive apartment complex on campus, you drove a Mercedes in your first weeks of school, and you wear name-brand clothes that even Audra, who comes from a wealthy family, couldn't afford."

"Appearances can be deceiving. I still think I'm worse off than you," Jewel said.

"No way," Kenny shook her head. "I'm the second of five siblings. My father was a haulage contractor, but he died in a road accident, leaving us devastated. We live in a modest three-bedroom house in a housing scheme. It's good that the house was semi-paid for before my dad died, or we would have been homeless.

"I only know Rory, Camden, because my mother was a teacher at that school, and my fees were heavily discounted. I probably wouldn't have met them if I hadn't gone there. But you look like you were born with a gold spoon in your mouth. When Audra and I first saw you, we thought you stepped off a luxurious magazine cover."

Jewel laughed. "As I said, appearances. It's all about appearances. My mother runs a club called Sensuous City and works for just above minimum wage. She had me when she was fifteen and in high school. My father wasn't much older. They were in the same class. They broke up around the same time my mother found out she was pregnant, and he denied being responsible.

"Unlike your dad, mine is alive, but he hasn't been a real presence in my life. He drives a taxi, which he owns, but he's always broke.

"I live with my mother in a two-bedroom bungalow on property belonging to her stepbrother. We own nothing."

Kenny opened her mouth in shock. "Say what?" she said.

"I'm not as fortunate as you to get a scholarship," Jewel sighed. "It seems getting one is all about connections. I live in the most expensive building on campus because my aunt pays for it, and she will pay as long as I get good grades. My step-uncle pays my school fees, and I have two years to repay him when I'm finished. He also loaned me one of his cars, but I sent it back It was too much of an expense for me."

"My clothes and shoes are all kind donations from my relatives who are scattered abroad," she continued.

"Are you serious?" Kenny whispered.

"Serious," Jewel replied. "At the end of the day, you're in a better position than I am."

"Oh wow," Kenny said, popping a grape in her mouth.

"And here I was envying you for your life."

"That's actually quite funny," Jewel snorted. "I was envying you for yours."

Kenny chuckled. "Your mother manages the notorious Sensuous City? I can't believe it. We were always warned that we had to do well in school or we'll end up at Sensuous City. It was never really that serious for me. Isn't Sensuous City where dancer Madge met DJ Duke?"

"Yes," Jewel said.

"DJ Duke is dreamy," Kenny licked her lips. "Have you ever met him in person?"

"Yes," Jewel nodded. "He's my mother's friend."

"Oh, my," Kenny was impressed. "I take it back; you have it better than me. You probably know all the local celebrities."

"I don't," Jewel grimaced. "When I go to Sensuous City, I'm not allowed to mingle with customers. My mother is quite protective."

"Imagine how different life would be if you had met one of those DJs who frequent the place," Kenny said dreamily. "He'd take one look at you, and then boom, your life would be sorted for the next couple of years."

"No thanks," Jewel said. "I'm determined to do it on my own."

"But you don't have to," Kenny said earnestly. "Look at how many men are offering to help you. If these gift baskets are any indication, you can make your life easier if you choose to."

"You sound like my mother," Jewel replied. "Getting help from men always comes with strings attached."

"I know, but you should still be able to handle it," Kenny said, finishing the grapes and heading for another basket with more grapes. "I'm going to Google their names and rank them according to net worth."

"No thanks," Jewel said, massaging her scalp gently. "I want to hear about Rory."

"You're serious about Rory, huh?" Kenny sat down on the settee, curling her feet under her. "I guess he could be a serious contender, given a few more years. He's still young and a student, but he has no money of his own, not that he's broke. Rory is from a rich family. His father owns Nelson Construction. You must have heard of them."

Jewel frowned doubtfully. "The name isn't strange."

"Well, they're rich, but they're also frugal. They don't flaunt their wealth, and all the children have to work. Rory has been working since he was quite young. I remember in high school, there was this fancy summer school program with horseback riding and trips to the beach, but Rory couldn't attend.

"His father had already booked him for the summer. I swear, he had to work, and Rory was already planning how to save up the money he made that summer and invest it in something his brother was involved in. We were only fourteen, and he was already talking about investments," Kenny said.

"That's not a bad thing," Jewel said. "It shows a strong work ethic and good money management skills."

"I guess," Kenny shrugged. "But if you want a smooth and easy life, why not try one of these very generous gift-givers? Choose the one who sent these grapes. These are nice grapes."

****

Rory didn't know why he was dithering outside of Jewel's door. He had a sketch that he had drawn of her, rolled up and tied with a bow. They had been texting each other for two weeks since the party, but they hadn't had a full conversation since then. Both of them had been busy with exams.

"I knew you would be bitten by the Jewel bug," Camden said as he came out of his apartment.

"It seems as if I've been," Rory grimaced.

"What's up?" Camden sneezed and stepped back. "I am coming down with something. It's probably from that last girl I kissed last night."

"How many girls were you kissing?" Rory asked incredulously.

"Three," Camden sniffled. "It was a party; they were freaky. I did things you are too innocent to hear about at this time."

"Make sure that the cold is the only thing you caught," Rory rolled his eyes.

"I know it is. I am being very careful in these streets," Camden groaned. "When are you going home?"

"I am going home in four days. My mom is coming to pick me up," Rory replied.

"We are spending Christmas in Miami with the grandparents," Camden sneezed again. "I am leaving tomorrow. I'll call you."

"Yup," Rory nodded.

"At least pretend like you care that I won't be around," Camden said. "You are salivating at her door like a kid at Christmas."

"I am not salivating," Rory chuckled.

"You are," Camden said as he knocked on the door and then ran down the hallway laughing.

Jewel opened the door seconds later and then gasped, "Rory."

"Both of us are exam free. Want to do something?" Rory

asked. He looked her up and down. She was dressed in short shorts and a tank top. Her belly was bare, flat, and defined. His eyes wandered down her legs and then up to her face.

Jewel laughed. "Come on in while I go change. What do you want to do?"

"I was thinking of going to a Christmas concert," Rory said as he stepped into Jewel's apartment and looked around. Gift baskets and flowers covered every available surface except her study desk.

"Wow," Rory said out loud.

"I keep getting presents and invitations to parties," Jewel said.

Rory leaned on the wall, feeling as if his present was inadequate compared to the display. He wondered why he had thrown himself into the fray of Jewel's admirers, as he had no idea it was so intense.

He looked at one of the flowers and saw a card that read, "To the lady in red from Ray Conrad."

"Ray Conrad," Rory sighed and stepped back. He realized that Jewel's admirers were leagues above him.

Jewel came out of the room in black jeans and a red sweater. She had brushed out her hair, and the curls hung down to her waist. She wasn't wearing any makeup. Rory's heart constricted. Sometimes he couldn't believe that she was talking to him and they were in regular contact.

"Well, here I am," Jewel smiled. "Let's go have some post-exam fun."

"When do you go home?" Rory asked.

Jewel shrugged, "I am in no hurry. Lester said I could spend Christmas with him and his girlfriend, but I don't want to be a third wheel."

"His girlfriend?" Rory chuckled. "I could swear I met his wife at the party a few weeks ago."

"Their relationship is strange," Jewel said. "Kristine will spend her time in Canada with the children and grandchildren, while Lester will be here with his friends. He splits his time between two female friends."

"So, what about your mother and father?" Rory asked.

"My mom works throughout the Christmas holidays," Jewel said. "Usually, I would split my time between my two grandmothers' houses in her absence, but my maternal grandmother doesn't spend much time here anymore. She's with my aunt in Cayman."

"As for my paternal grandmother," Jewel continued, "she usually hosts a large Christmas gathering. If I go there before Christmas day, I'll be worked like crazy. I'm in the mood to take it easy this year."

"I understand," Rory laughed. "Let's have fun this Christmas. We'll hang out."

"I am game," Jewel nodded.

"We'll plan it," Rory said. "Go on different adventures."

"I don't have a car," Jewel said. "I sent it back to my uncle. I can't maintain such a luxury vehicle on my university allowance."

Rory nodded, "That's smart. My mom will pick me up in four days with my new vehicle. You can come along, and we'll spend the whole vacation together. My parents have a house in Cascade Hills. I'll spend most of my time there, it's close enough to where you live. It'll be fun."

Jewel nodded, "Okay."

Rory handed her the sketch. "And this is for you. I would have stepped up my game if I had known the competition was sending flowers, chocolate, and wine."

Jewel took the paper and gasped, "It's me!"

Rory nodded, "Yes, it is."

"You're good. It's really nice," Jewel smiled at him. "I'm

going to frame it."

Rory let out a sigh of relief, seeing that she liked it.

"You should do one of us," Jewel said as she linked arms with him. "Let's go have an adventure."

****

Rory knew things wouldn't go well with his mother and Jewel from the moment he introduced them, and his mother saw her and heard her surname.

His mother, who was usually friendly and welcoming to all his friends, gave Jewel a cold hello and told her to call her Mrs. Nelson.

He saw Jewel reeling from the snub, but he couldn't do anything about it. He had offered her a ride to her house, but his mother had brought the vehicle, and he had unfortunately not mentioned the topic of Lester Webb and his connection to his mother.

They were too busy having fun and getting to know each other, and he didn't think to bring up his mother's past with her cousin.

As he drove out of campus, he regretted not finding the time to mention it. His mother turned to look at Jewel in the back seat and asked, "So, Jewel, where exactly are you from in Trelawny?"

"Cascade Hills," Jewel said brightly.

"And what do your parents do?" his mother continued.

Rory stopped at a stoplight and turned to look at Jewel. "You don't have to answer that. Mom, stop giving Jewel the third degree. For now, she's just a friend. I don't want you to scare her away. I have some tough competition working with; she's every guy's fantasy."

Jewel laughed. "But I like you, which puts you at the front

of the line."

"I really wish you wouldn't put him at the front of your line," Bunny said, not finding it funny. "Rory is too young for a serious relationship. Girls like you should come with a warning label, glamorous heartbreaker."

"Mom, stop," Rory grunted.

He was seriously annoyed. He hoped Bunny could hear it in his voice and see it on his face. Luckily, her phone rang. There was a crisis at the office, so she went into office manager mode for most of the trip.

Jewel fell asleep for most of the way, and he answered in monosyllables as his mother attempted conversation between her phone calls.

It was only when they were in the middle of Falmouth, the main town in Trelawny, that Jewel woke up and murmured, "Could you drop me at Sensuous City? I don't want to take you out of your way to go up to Cascade Hills."

Bunny's eyebrows almost shot up into her hairline. "Why ever would you be going to that godawful place?"

"My mother manages it," Jewel said, unaware of the shock she was causing. They had never gone into much detail about their families in all their talks.

Bunny looked at him significantly and then looked straight ahead. He knew what was running through his mother's mind: Jewel wasn't good enough.

For once, he didn't care what his mother thought. "I'll call you," he said as she got out of the car.

Jewel looked at him doubtfully. She had felt the vibes his mother was giving off, and she wasn't hopeful that they would be connecting over the holidays.

He could see all the thoughts running through her mind. It was physically hurting him to leave her at that moment. They had connected in the last four days.

"No, Rory," Bunny said firmly. "Don't even think about that girl. Of all the girls at the university, you chose her from Lester Webb's family. A girl whose mother manages the secret brothel in town. What kind of upbringing does she have? I shiver to think of her morals and values."

"How do you know she's from Lester's family?" Rory asked. "Webb is a common surname."

"Because she looks like his sister Octavia and she's from Cascade Hills," Bunny replied. "I grew up with all of them, remember? I'm assuming she's related to one of Edna's boys. Back in the day, all the girls wanted to be with them. They were all good-looking men, unapologetic womanizers. Lester was the worst of them, a male gold digger who didn't bat an eye at cheating on his wife."

"Mom, that's all in the past," Rory said, gripping the steering wheel tightly. "What Lester did to you was terrible. Unfortunately, people cheat and hurt their partners. Before you knew he was a cheater, you loved him because he was nice. He still is. His behavior has nothing to do with Jewel. She's not Lester. She's her own person with her own way of doing things. I'm sure you wouldn't want to be judged based on your family."

"How do you know how nice Lester Webb is?" Bunny asked, ignoring most of Rory's defense of Jewel and focusing on Lester.

"I went to his housewarming party," Rory said, glancing at Bunny. "He instantly recognized me."

Bunny had a look of contemplation on her face, wondering how she would punish him. "So, Jewel has been pulling you into Lester's circle, has she?"

"No," Rory said. "Lester was the one who introduced us. We live on the same floor in the same building, but it took an invitation to his party for us to meet. He introduced us."

"I wonder what his purpose is," Bunny said, musing. "Is he trying to get to me through her?"

"I doubt it," Rory groaned. "Mom, this might hurt, but I don't think Lester has thought about you much in the last thirty years. He has a wife and two girlfriends. I don't think he'd have a vendetta against an ex from so long ago."

"I don't know what he's plotting and planning," Bunny said. "Lester is pure evil, and she's evil adjacent. Do me a favor, and don't see her anymore."

"I can't promise that," Rory said honestly. "I think I'm falling in love with her."

"You don't know what love is," Bunny scoffed. "She's got a pretty face and a nice body. You have a crush; that's expected. This will sort itself out. I have no idea why I'm even worried about her. If she's anything like her family, she'll soon dump you for someone who is older and not limited by their allowance."

Rory winced but didn't argue. He had that same fear in the last four days. He would have to work extra hard this holiday to ensure she didn't see anyone else.

Chapter Six

"**M**y university student is here!" Pearl bellowed as Jewel walked into the semi-dark interior of the club behind the delivery men stacking crates of drinks. The club section wouldn't open until five that evening, but the bar was open, and a few patrons were there.

"Hey, Jewel!" several of the delivery guys greeted her. Many of them had known her since she was little.

Tony, the bartender, grinned. "One semester down, five to go."

"Hey, Tony," Jewel smiled.

"What do you want to drink to celebrate?" Tony asked.

"Ginger and juice," Jewel replied.

"I see you haven't changed," Tony grinned. "This has been your standard order since you were twelve years old."

"And it will be her standard order when she's eighty," Pearl said, unconcerned about her customers overhearing. "Alcohol ages and weakens your faculties. How are you, baby?"

"Fine-ish," Jewel grimaced. She was still upset because of Bunny Nelson's attitude and worried that Rory would think she wasn't good enough.

Pearl kissed Jewel on the cheek. "Wait for me in the office. I'm coming to hear what's put the 'ish' in your 'fine.' I have to make sure these men aren't scamming me. It's Christmas time. Everybody's a scammer."

Jewel took her drink from Tony and headed to Pearl's office. It was spacious, with a bathroom, shower, pull-out couch, and desk. The latest prominent picture on the desk was of Jewel and Pearl at her high school graduation.

Jewel circumvented the desk and sank down into the couch. There were nights when she had slept on the couch while she waited for Pearl to finish an event because she had to stay back to lock up after the last patron left. Jewel had truly learned to sleep through any noise because of Sensuous City.

Pearl, as usual, had a stack of books in a bookcase nearby. Jewel got up and perused the titles. Pearl was unashamedly a romance lover; her book titles tended to all have the same theme, The Millionaires Love, The Billionaires Caress, and the Rich Man's Bride. Pearl was not going to read about an ordinary man living an everyday life, falling in love, and getting on with life.

Nope, that was not her style.

Jewel chuckled. Even her non-fiction titles were telling. How to Be A Millionaire in a Year, How I Made a Killing in the Stock Market, App 101: Build Apps Make Money.

Jewel drew that one from the bookcase. This one was more up her alley. She wondered why Pearl had it. She wasn't particularly technologically savvy.

She started reading and sipping on her ginger and juice.

Tony had added bitters to it, which gave it a kick. It was really good.

"So what's got you fine-ish?" Pearl entered the office.

"Nothing really," Jewel said, looking up from her book. "I met a guy, and I like him."

"Is he rich?" Pearl asked.

"No, but his parents are," Jewel said. "He's a student."

Pearl sighed. "I guess that's not all bad news."

"His mother hated me on sight," Jewel said. "I could just tell. She took one look at me, and bam, the resentment hit me in the face."

"Why would she hate you?" Pearl asked incredulously. "Everybody loves you. It's a given."

"I don't think she got the memo," Jewel said. "Maybe she doesn't consider me good enough for her son."

"Who is this woman?" Pearl sat down at her desk with a thunderous expression.

"Bonita Nelson," Jewel said. "The boy I like is Rory Nelson."

"Ah, Miss Bunny," Pearl mused. "Bobby Nelson's wife. She's helped more than a few girls here who have gotten into trouble. I always thought she was a good person. She's one of those rare society ladies who's always willing to help and doesn't put on any airs. Girls are usually comfortable approaching her for anything."

"She can be a good person and dislike me at the same time," Jewel shrugged. "I doubt she'll let me see Rory this holiday."

"Mmmm," Pearl was in deep thought. "I wonder if her dislike has anything to do with the rumors that her first son is Lester's kid."

"Lester?" Jewel sat up in the chair. "Of course, he told me about Bonita and his son, Jeremiah. I never made the connection. That's it. She was smiling until I told her my name was Jewel Webb. Then, it was as if a shutter came over her face."

"I should have just given you my surname," Jewel said. "Jewel Day sounds better than Jewel Webb. Darnell doesn't deserve his name being attached to yours anyway."

Jewel laughed, a sense of heady relief overtaking her, so it wasn't anything that she had done that had caused Bunny Nelson to dislike her. It was just her history with Lester.

"Forget about her and her son," Pearl said flippantly. "You can do better than the last son of a rich man who's still in school. You need an established rich man with a seat at the table, not someone still in a highchair."

Jewel shook her head. "I knew this would be your response," she said.

"I'm practical and unromantic," Pearl replied. "I'm trying to drive any notion of romance out of your head. Your life would be better without it."

"Lester married for money, and he's not happy with Kristine," Jewel pointed out. "I am not like you. I still believe in romance and happily ever after and that you can find the person you click with and be reasonably happy in this life. Sorry to tell you, Mom, but your cynical attitude did not take. My ideals can't be exorcised like you've been trying to do for the past nineteen years."

"You'll learn," Pearl grunted. "Anyway, what are you doing for the holiday?"

"I don't know," Jewel shrugged. "I was planning to visit Grandma Edna's house on Christmas Day."

Pearl nodded. "Make sure you visit Pastor Brewster. He's not feeling well, and his arthritis is acting up."

"Of course," Jewel said, nodding. "I'll visit him tomorrow."

"I'll be sleeping over here on Christmas night," Pearl said.

"As usual," Jewel replied with a weary smile.

"Ladies!" Leonard popped his head around the office door. "The university student is here."

"Hello, Uncle Leonard," Jewel said, giving him a smile.

Leonard Crooks was large, a towering figure, standing well over six feet tall and broad-shouldered. He shaved his hair to hide the greys, and his bald head glistened in the office light.

The richer he got, the less exercise he indulged in; his belly was rounder than Jewel could remember seeing it, and his medium brown complexion, which was relatively smooth, had more pot marks than Jewel could remember him having.

"So, how is it going?" he asked.

"I'm doing well, thank you. I'm just home for the Christmas break."

"Good, good," Leonard said, nodding approvingly. "And how was your first semester? Everything on track?"

"It was okay; more work than I anticipated," Jewel said. "I'm so grateful for your support. I don't know how I would have been able to afford college without your help."

Leonard grinned. "Nonsense. You're a bright young woman with a lot of potential. I'm just glad I can help you reach your goals.

"Now, Pearl," Leonard turned to her and frowned fiercely. "I heard from Leona that you're refusing to share some champagne with the restaurant. The suppliers say they won't be able to fulfill her orders for three days, and you can give her some."

"And I explained to her that I have too many events in the days ahead to share," Pearl said. "Did she think running to you would change my mind?"

"She did," Leonard said. "I did say I would come by and

throw my weight around on her behalf."

"The answer is still no," Pearl said firmly. "tell Leona that I make precise orders based on the demand here. I'm not being selfish. I have too many events to lend my liquor. We all know that everyone has to order well in advance of this time of year."

Leonard nodded. "Well, okay then. I'll have to figure out how to save an event we have tonight at the restaurant."

"Good luck with that," Pearl said.

Leonard grunted and left the office.

Jewel chuckled. "You really know how to handle that man."

"I don't," Pearl said. "This club makes more money than the restaurant, and he knows that. He also knows that I don't mess around when it comes to the bottom line. His little performance just now was a test. If I had given him the liquor, he would call me soft and claim that I am losing my edge. I'm used to that man. He runs his businesses like a mini competition. Somebody should bring a camera up here. We'd make for a good show."

****

Jewel drove to the house that night and looked over at a sleepy Pearl. "We are home."

The cottage stood cute and quaint in the half-dark. It was painted white with green trimmings. Its humble façade was a far cry from their neighbor Leonard's house, which was above them on a hill.

It was four stories high and quite wide. You could catch glimpses of it through the pine trees surrounding the edifice. Leonard had inherited five acres of land from his father and had bought a few more acres from his other brothers and sister, who no longer resided in Jamaica.

He had the bulk share of his father's estate, and his stepmother, who was also Pearl's mother and Jewel's grandmother, was allowed to live in the original family house until she died according to the will, but after her husband died two years ago, she started spending most of her time with her daughter in Cayman.

Jewel didn't blame her. It had gotten tense in the family as everybody jostled for their share of the inheritance pie. Leonard had been the only one who had brought some calm to the proceedings. He had bought them out to control it all, and he had gotten his siblings to lay off their stepmother.

They owed Leonard more than just for the cottage he had built for Pearl or her university education. If it weren't for him, her grandmother would have had nowhere to live when her husband died.

"What time is it?" Pearl asked.

"Near midnight," Jewel replied. "Early for you."

"You know what I'd like?" Pearl said hoarsely. "A 9-to-5. I don't understand why people complain about it. What's not to love? You get up, go to work, come back home when it's still evening, and leave work behind. Then you do it all again the next day. Instead, I work from midday and come home at 9 in the morning, sometimes later, and I do it every day of the week."

Jewel chuckled. "I'm surprised you came up here with me."

"I finally convinced Leonard to hire someone to help me out," Pearl said. "He sent over Trixie."

"One of his exes?" Jewel asked.

"Oh, yes, a recent ex, too," Pearl snorted. "She's sometimes annoying. She thinks she and Leonard will get back together, and that's all she talks about, but I appreciate her otherwise.

She's a hard worker. I'm training her to replace me."

"You are?" Jewel gasped. "You've never said a word."

"I have plans," Pearl said. "I'm tired of this lifestyle. I want out. I want to be free of Leonard and Sensuous City, but it takes planning. That's all I'm going to say about it. I want you to have plausible deniability when I leave."

Jewel opened the front door, and they entered the cozy living room. All the furniture was paid for by Leonard and, thankfully, was neutral in color, as Pearl had decorated the entire place in shades of purple, from the palest lavender to lilac and mauve. She had not strayed from that palette at all. Even the focal picture was of a woman sitting in profile with swirls of purple around her. It worked, or at least Jewel had gotten used to it. It felt like home.

"Goodnight," Jewel said to Pearl.

"Night," Pearl murmured, "I'm happy you're home."

She headed straight to her room, staggering from exhaustion.

Jewel sat on the couch with her bag at her feet. She wasn't feeling sleepy; she had slept on the way down and taken a nap in Sensuous City. She couldn't wait to call Rory. It was strange how much he had come to mean to her.

What was it about certain people that made you so aware of them? You didn't know they existed one minute, and the next, they were all you could think about. Maybe he was sleeping. She texted him to make sure. "Hey."

"Hey," he texted back almost immediately.

"I thought you weren't talking to me after today. I forgot to tell you my mother runs Sensuous City. I think I shocked your mom."

"She'll get over it," Rory responded. "What are you doing tomorrow?"

"Visiting a retired friend and shopping."

"I'll visit and shop with you. Give me directions to your place." Jewel happily entered the directions, grinning as she did so. He still liked her and wanted to spend time together. This was shaping up to be the best Christmas ever.

Chapter Seven

Rory hadn't slept much the night before. It always took him a moment to adjust to a bed. His old bed and his room which had always been a familiar place, his sanctuary, now felt strange and new. He had only left it for three months, and already he had to be readjusting.

After texting Jewel, he had called her, and they had talked way into the early hours. He wasn't supposed to be up now. Usually, he would be taking a lie in, but he was psyched and ready to go and spend time with her.

His parents were already at the breakfast table with his brothers.

Mercedes sauntered in after he shared out his food. She had her camera around her neck.

"I just love when the family is together," Bunny said pleasantly. "Any general family updates?"

"I have to go back to work the day after Christmas," Larry said grumpily. "Why don't you come home and work with the family?" Bobby asked. "We would welcome you with open arms."

"Not ready to come back home yet," Larry said, then glanced at him to change the subject. "Did you grow an extra inch since I saw you in summer? You look bigger, taller, more like a man, less like a boy."

"You may be onto something, Larry," Jeremiah chimed in. "He became a man overnight."

"I look the same," Rory laughed.

"Nope," Mercedes said. "I was just looking through some pictures of you. Maturity has arrived. Your muscles even look more masculine. Spill the tea; all the girls swoon when they see you, don't they?"

"No," Rory grinned. "But thanks for the compliment, though."

"He has an admirer," Bunny said. "Quite a pretty girl. I told him to stay away from her; she'll break his heart."

"Is that so?" Bobby raised an eyebrow. "You actually managed to tear yourself from your computer to pull a pretty girl?"

"Yes, Rory, do tell," Mercedes grinned.

"I like her very, very, very much," Rory stressed. "And when I bring her around, I don't want any of you to make her feel uncomfortable."

"You're not bringing her around," Bunny said through clenched teeth. "Didn't we agree that you would stay away from her?"

"I didn't agree to that," Rory said. "You said it. I silently listened."

"Ooh," Mercedes grinned, "He is indeed growing up, defying his mommy."

"But Rory…" Bunny protested.

"Leave the boy, Bunny," Bobby said. "When I was his

age, if my parents told me to stop seeing someone, that's when I would see them. If you really want him to leave her, you should welcome her with open arms, befriend her, and become besties."

"Her mother runs Sensuous City," Bunny said through clenched teeth.

"The den of iniquity," Larry gasped, imitating, clutching his imaginary pearls.

Jeremiah and Mercedes hooted with laughter.

"Running a nightclub is running a business," Rory winced. "I don't see what the problem is."

"Oh, really now," Bunny snorted. "You know the kinds of debauchery that take place in those places."

"I had no idea my mother was a snob," Larry chuckled. "So many years on this planet, and I am finally finding this out."

"Mom is no snob," Jeremiah defended Bunny. "There must be something else. Does the pretty girl work at Sensuous City, by any chance?"

"No," Rory said exasperatedly. "She goes to the same school I go to and lives on the same floor. She's your cousin."

"My cousin?" Jeremiah frowned. "And not your cousin?"

Rory nodded. "She's related to Lester Webb."

"Ah," Jeremiah glanced at his mother. "There lies the reason for the snobbery. My sperm donor is involved."

"It's quite interesting," Mercedes said. "Mom loves you but hates your biological father, and that hate extends to this girl but not you. There must be something in psychology to define this. I have to look it up. This is fascinating."

"The girl's name is Jewel," Rory said. "Jewel Webb."

"I'd like to meet her," Jeremiah said. "I don't really know that side of the family. Haven't had the interest to know them, really."

"I'd like to meet her too," Mercedes said. "I like her name."

"Me too," Larry chuckled. "Invite her over for Christmas dinner."

"Listen," Bunny said through gritted teeth. "I don't like this. Larry only wants her over because he likes chaos and drama."

"I wouldn't mind meeting her either," Bobby said, looking at his wife pointedly. "Let it go, Bunny. The past is in the past."

"I have let it go," Bunny tried to state calmly. "Christmas dinner will be at my parents' house; we can't possibly allow her to impose."

"We invite people every year, even off the streets, and the fact that it's in Cascade Hills is even better. It's close to where she lives." Rory smiled.

Bunny made a garbled groaning sound, so Rory knew it was time to make his exit. He glanced at his watch, it was nearly nine, and he had promised to take Jewel to visit her retired friend and do some shopping.

"I'm going," he said as he stood up. "I promised Jewel I would take her to see her pastor."

"Wait, you're going to see a pastor?" Larry chuckled. "Does this mean you're getting married so soon? You just met her, right?"

"Over my dead body," Bunny glared at him.

"No, we're not getting married," Rory chuckled. "She's just visiting. She and her mom lived with the pastor and his wife when she was a baby, and they remained close. The pastor is ailing, so Jewel wants to visit. I don't want to be late. Bye, guys."

"Ah, young love," Jeremiah said.

"It doesn't always work out," Larry said wistfully. "But

when it does, it's glorious."

"Don't forget we need your help on the House Builders Charity project," Bobby said gruffly. "We need everyone's help so the family we're helping can move in for Christmas."

"I'll take Jewel along," Rory nodded.

"If she wants to get her hands dirty, that's fine by me." Bobby nodded.

"That girl won't want to work on a construction site," Bunny perked up. "Tell her it's for charity, and everyone there is a volunteer. Let's see what she's made of."

****

"I'd love to come and work on the charity project," Jewel said excitedly when Rory finally brought up the question after they left her pastor friend's house. They had spent more time there than Rory anticipated. The Brewsters were entertaining.

Pastor Brewster had served in ministry for over fifty years and was now retired and in his seventies. He spent much of his time growing orchids. Jewel found it difficult to leave because he didn't want to stop once he started talking about his extensive collection. He gave Jewel a plant with three spikes of deep purple flowers as her Christmas present.

"Where do we go now?" Rory asked.

Jewel smiled. "I want to stop at Nessa's and get a gift for my mom." "So, that means a late lunch?"

Rory sighed. "I'm used to women having long shopping sprees."

Jewel giggled. "My mom visits Nessa at least once a month and always raves about the clothes and perfumes she likes. I'll just ask Nessa what she liked last time and get that. My mom is the easiest person to shop for."

Rory grinned. "Makes sense."

"It will be fun working for a charity," Jewel said. "Thank you for asking me."

"It's on a construction site," Rory warned. "I don't know what's left to do there. We have two weeks to go before Christmas Eve, which is when they want to do the handover to the family. We might have to pull some all-nighters."

"Sounds fun," Jewel said. "I have some old clothes I don't mind discarding after this. I didn't want to just dump them. You know, they were too old to give away and too ratty to wear in public, so this is perfect."

Rory laughed. "My mother said you wouldn't want to do anything like this."

"She doesn't know me," Jewel said. "I'm hoping we can get to know each other better, and she can stop assuming things about me just because I'm related to the Webbs."

"I hope so, too," Rory nodded. "By the way, you're invited to Christmas dinner."

"Oh, really?" Jewel smiled. "That's like throwing me in the deep end. I'm not even your girlfriend yet. They may scare me off, and I won't want to have anything to do with you after dinner."

"I know," Rory said. "But my siblings are excited to meet you."

"So, you've been talking about me, huh?"

Rory nodded. "I have. Is that a problem?"

"No," Jewel laughed. "I think I like it."

****

"This is the best Christmas ever!" Jewel said, as she sat beside him in her paint covered clothes.

All of the volunteers were beat.

It was a little after nine in the evening, and they had just finished cleaning up the house, which would be handed over to the new family just in time for Christmas Eve. They had worked nonstop all day clearing the yard and inside the house. The twelve of them were on the back veranda waiting for their catered food arrived from Silver Spoon Restaurant.

Jewel sat in a circle with Rory and his siblings, all of whom had pitched in to work to make the project happen.

"For a newbie, you really worked hard," Larry said admiringly, "You have a good eye for interior design. I liked your paint choices. I won't forget that you like green and grey."

"Thank you," Jewel nodded. "Coming from you, that's high praise, Larry, because I think you are amazingly creative."

"He is not all that," Rory murmured.

Larry laughed. "I am too hungry to rebut."

"I am starving," Mercedes mumbled, "I would eat a cow."

"I saw one up the road," Jeremiah grunted.

"But I am too hungry to get up and go eat him," Mercedes leaned her head on his shoulder. "Go get him for me."

"I would," Jeremiah said, "but I am too old for that sort of thing; ask Rory. He is a stropping, young, energetic lad. He can build a house and hunt a cow all with one hand tied behind him."

Jewel giggled.

Rory sighed. "I agree with all that, but hunting a cow and eating it as is would take the concept of rare beef to unpalatable levels, and I am concerned for your digestive system."

They all laughed.

Jewel moved closer to him; even though she was sweaty and sticky and probably smelled, she wanted to be closer to him. She liked him. Two weeks of seeing him, working together to build something amazing, had cemented her attraction to him even more. And he had worked hard; now she knew why he was so muscular.

He could do everything. He chipped in with the tiling and carpentry and installed cupboards and doors. He fixed flaws that Jewel had no idea were there, but he and his brothers found appalling.

She had been paired with Mercedes and a few of the other girls with the painting and the clean-up work. They did a decent job of it; the place was clean as a whistle and move-in ready.

Jewel was amazed that Nelson Construction had completed a two-bedroom house in three months and only with volunteers. Jeremiah had overseen the first phase of the project, and Larry had taken over for the last stages.

She loved the sibling dynamic among them. They worked like a well-oiled machine. They frequently joked with each other and sometimes acted ridiculous, but by and large, they were quite serious about giving back.

Rory told her that their family financed and worked on a housing project three times each year.

All of them chipped in to help, and Nelson Construction provided the resources. And now a lucky family was going to have a house. She was touched by it and impressed by them.

"So, is there going to be a handing-over ceremony?" Jewel asked.

"Yes," Rory answered, "tomorrow, the movers will bring the furniture."

"Oh my," Jewel asked, "they get furniture too?"

"Oh yes, they get everything," Mercedes said. "Their previous place was flooded, their house washed into the gully, they have nothing. We work with other charities to give them a second chance. So two other charities will come on board tomorrow. Now that the house is finished, they'll stock this place with furniture, clothes, bedding, and food."

"And toys," Jeremiah said. "This place will be given to a single mother with three children under five. Her husband died in the flood. He was trying to rescue someone caught in the current, but he also lost his life."

Jewel blinked away tears.

Rory squeezed her hand. "You, okay?"

"I heard the story on the news. I didn't know this was for that family. My mom and I donated clothes," Jewel said.

"And so many people donated their time and resources," Mercedes said, "to make this place habitable for them. The world might be going to the dogs, but our sense of community still works."

Jewel swiped her eyes. "Give me a minute; this is making me emotional."

"Beautiful and empathetic," Larry murmured. "She's a keeper, Rory."

"I know," Rory looked at her. "Do you want my clean shirt to dry your eyes?"

Jewel chuckled. "I am good."

The food came shortly after that; they ate and joked around. When Rory dropped her home, it was after midnight

"I think we earned a vacation," Rory said. "Maybe we should do something non-taxing tomorrow. I'll pick you up; we can hang out at the Cascade Hill house. We'll watch television and eat."

Jewel nodded. "Sure. Sounds like a vacation."

"I'll pick you up around midday," Rory reached across and kissed her briefly. "See you tomorrow."

Jewel smiled. He kissed her; her lips still tingled.

"See you tomorrow."

Chapter Eight

"**S**o, you're the famous Rory?"

"Yes, I am," Rory nodded in bemusement as a girl who looked slightly older than Jewel answered the front door when he got there. "And you are?"

"Pearl Day, Jewel's mom," she said as she looked him over. "She never said you were so handsome."

She never said you looked so young, Rory thought to himself, still surprised by Pearl's appearance. He had expected her to look like a brothel madam, with heavy makeup and maybe an ill-fitting wig; she should be dropping out of her too-tight clothes. He laughed inwardly, where had he gotten that image from?

Pearl looked like an ordinary girl in the streets. She was dressed in jeans and a t-shirt. She was slim but curvy and was around the same height as Jewel. Her face was make-up-free, and her hair was cut in a short pixie cut that flattered her oval-shaped face.

When Jewel entered the living room, she smiled at Rory. "So, you found the place, okay?"

"It wasn't hard; your uncle's house is the biggest in Cascade Hills. I just drove toward it," Rory replied.

Jewel nodded. "I knew it would be a landmark."

"Okay, I'm going," Pearl interjected, kissing Jewel and looking at Rory again. "Be good, both of you."

Rory nodded, "Yes, ma'am."

After Pearl left the house, Rory looked at Jewel incredulously. "That's really your mom? She had you when you were what, three?"

"Yes, that's my mom," Jewel laughed. "She had me when she was fifteen, but all the women on her side of the family are young-looking. You should see my great-grandmother; she still looks youthful."

"I see," Rory nodded. "That's good to know."

"Here's an album," Jewel laughed as she reached down to the bottom of a bookshelf and pulled out two huge albums. "I hope you don't have other plans because there are many pictures."

"No, I don't," Rory laughed. "I just want to hang with you today. Are you coming to the family Christmas dinner thingy with me tomorrow?"

"Sure," Jewel nodded. "I'll be here alone if I don't tag along. That's no fun. Last Christmas, I watched Home Alone reruns, ate supermarket-bought fruitcake and sorrel, and made myself a chicken sandwich. I had been too lazy to go up in the hills to Grandma Edna's house. My dad had offered to pick me up, but then he had a last-minute change of plans, and I didn't want to inconvenience anybody else. How did you spend your Christmas?"

"It was great," Rory shrugged. "It's the same every year. We eat at my grandparents'; there's enough food to feed an army. We play games, chat, and eat again. Usually, we stay at our Cascade Hill house and repeat the next day. It's fun. Sometimes our cousins will bunk over with us, and we'll have quite a fun time."

"Well, then, I am looking forward to that this year," Jewel said. "I'm so happy I met you."

"You know what? Me too," Rory winked at her.

****

Their plans to stay at his family home, located behind his grandparent's house, and watch movies and chill were disrupted when evening rolled around. Rory's uncle Mike stopped by the Cascade Hills house. He had arrived from Canada the evening before and was eager to hit the streets.

He greeted Jewel as if he had always known her, embraced his nephew in a bear hug, and started chatting.

"I heard you have your own vehicle now, young Rory," Mike said.

Rory nodded, "It's parked outside."

"Good, I saw it," Mike grinned. "What are you two doing this evening?"

"Watching television, snacking, just hanging," Rory replied.

"But you can do that anytime," Mike protested. "It's Christmas Eve. You two can't just chill. Let's go out, walk around, eat jerk chicken at the side of the road, stop at various street dances, and have fun! Come on, nephew, take your pretty girlfriend, and let's go."

Rory looked at Jewel. "Do you want us to venture out?"

Jewel shrugged, "Not really. I used to walk around when I was younger, but it was boring."

"Because you didn't do it Mikey style," Mike grinned. "I

want to relive a Jamaican Christmas with Fiona. You'll get on like a house on fire with her, Jewel."

"What he means is he needs a designated driver," Rory grumbled. "Because he'll be stopping at every Tom, Dick, and Harry's house and drinking to cheer on Christmas."

"Atta boy," Mike grinned. "I knew Bunny never raised a fool. Let's go; time is running out."

It was 9 o'clock when Jewel, Mike, and his wife Fiona piled into Rory's vehicle and headed for the town.

Jewel had expected it to be boring, but Fiona and Mike were entertaining and thrill-seekers. They acted like teenagers who had just escaped their parents, not forty-something adults with children. Jewel and Rory felt like the adults.

It was the most fun Jewel could remember having, and she hadn't laughed so hard in her life.

Mike knew everybody, it seemed. They stopped at four parties and were greeted warmly. They were offered food and sorrel drinks laced with liquor.

"My mother would be disappointed to see me drinking this," Jewel said after a particularly spiked drink.

"It's the season," Mike said joyfully. "Drink up."

He hauled his wife into a tight embrace, and they danced up a storm to the booming sounds of the sound box nearby.

"Whose yard is this?" Jewel shouted to Rory, as she could barely hear over the music.

Rory chuckled. "Uncle Mike's friend, Lenny." His lips were on her ear, sending a tingle down her spine.

She pulled back a little. "Let's go to the car. It's warmer in there," Rory pulled her closer.

They went into the car where the music wasn't as loud, and Jewel bopped her head to the song currently playing, "If I Had the World" by Dennis Brown.

"Love this song," Rory said.

"Then let's go dance to it," Jewel said, opening the car door again. "It's not right for your uncle Mike to have more fun than us. He's old. We are the teenagers!"

They danced the night away. It was almost five o'clock in the morning when Rory drove up to the house. Mike and Fiona decided to sleep over instead of waking up the house next door, and Rory invited Jewel to stay too.

Jewel couldn't say no. She was tired but also needed to shower, as she smelled like roasted breadfruit and smoke.

Rory showed her the toiletries. Everything was packaged in little bags: mini shampoos and toothbrushes.

"Goodnight," Rory came to the door after she was snuggled up in bed, trying to find a warm spot. The house was chilly. This section of Cascade Hills was noticeably chillier than where she lived.

"You mean good morning?" Jewel said, her mouth trembling. "My body will punish me for this tomorrow, that is if I can sleep. It's so cold."

"I'll warm you up," Rory said as he climbed into the bed with her, pressing his body on hers. The trembling calmed down, giving way to a new tremor.

"Are you warm yet?" Rory asked.

Jewel turned to him. "I am getting there."

"You smell so good," Rory said.

"You too," Jewel whispered.

Jewel didn't know who made the first move, but their lips were close together, and it was only natural that they pressed them to each other. It started as an exploratory kiss and ended up heated.

Rory's hands were on her bare breast before she realized that her top was off, and her hands were splayed on his chest.

"We have to stop," Rory said hoarsely, stopping the never-ending kiss. "I have no protection with me, and I don't want my first time to be in a house with Uncle Mike across the hall."

"Yes," Jewel looked at him dazedly.

"We are combustible together," Rory said.

Jewel shouted "Yes" inwardly. Now she knew what losing one's inhibitions meant. Now she knew how people could throw caution to the wind and bring unwanted babies into the world. "I'll go to the other room," Rory said. "I can't stay in here with you."

"I understand," Jewel said hoarsely, finally finding her voice.

"See you later," Rory kissed her forehead and groaned. "Now I don't know if I'll be able to get much sleep."

****

He slept. The clock was saying noon when he popped one eye open.

Somebody was whispering over his head to the right of him. They didn't know he was awake. He finally worked out that it was his mother and his father.

"I can't believe he carried that girl into my home," Bunny hissed. "Up here, at Cascade Hills."

"Bunny, you need to tone down your dislike for this girl. Maybe she has come into your life to help you move on. She is not Octavia. She is Jewel."

"Why, of all the girls at university, did Rory choose her?" Bunny asked. "I tell you, the Webb family is a bane to my existence."

"The Webb family is also a blessing," Bobby replied. "We have Jeremiah because of Lester, and, in a roundabout way, we have Mercedes because of Octavia."

"Mom, Dad," Rory said, turning around on the bed. "They were both dressed up. His mother was in a red flowing dress, and his father was in a long-sleeved red and white striped shirt."

"He's awake," Bunny said gruffly. "Your uncle Mike said you made quite a lively foursome last night. Fiona and your 'friend' are still sleeping."

"We did have fun," Rory nodded.

"It's almost time for the official dinner. If you're going to invite your 'friend' to come along, you should get up and have her get dressed. Dinner is at two."

"What does Mercedes have to do with Octavia?" Rory asked, confused. "And why are you referring to Jewel as my friend like that?"

"Mercedes has nothing to do with Octavia," Bunny said quickly. "And isn't Jewel your friend?"

"Come on, Bunny," Bobby said. "Let's leave him to it. Don't come by too late, Rory."

"Wait!" Rory sat up in bed and rubbed his eyes. "What are you not telling me?"

"If I tell you," Bunny said, "would you leave Jewel alone forever?"

"No," Rory frowned. "Is it something she did?"

"She didn't do a thing," Bobby replied. "Your mother needs to work through some past things. Let's go, Bunny."

****

Jewel was beside herself with excitement. Rory had dropped her home to shower and change into a party dress. He had gotten ready at home a few minutes before and had taken her to get ready at her place, which was only ten minutes away from Rory's parents' place. He was waiting patiently for her in the living room.

She knew the dress she would wear - a red, long-sleeved knit dress that fit the holiday theme. It was too warm for the summer but perfect for this cooler weather. Rifling through her closet didn't take long. She showered, washed her hair, and gave it a quick blow dry, enough so her curls wouldn't be dripping.

She looked at herself in the mirror critically. No need for makeup today, just a little lip gloss. Rory looked at her appreciatively when she stepped out of the room. "You look gorgeous, as usual," he said.

Rory was scrolling through her childhood album when she came out. "Who are these people?" he asked.

"That's my grandmother, Edna, on her wedding day when she was about seventeen. The handsome chap beside her is my grandfather Reese. They were both seventeen. They made for a good-looking couple, didn't they?"

"They do look good together," Rory nodded. "Seventeen is so young to get married, though."

"If you think seventeen is too young, Reid and Nellie are the couple on the other page, they got married at sixteen."

"Reese and Reid look like the same person," Rory squinted at the album. "And Edna and Nellie look alike."

"I know. Reid and Reese are identical twins, and Edna and Nellie are sisters. Edna is my grandmother, and Nellie is Lester's mom."

"Oh wow," Rory said. "Edna and Reese had six boys, and Nellie and Reid had two children, Lester and Octavia."

"I see," Rory nodded.

"I could swear I told you this yesterday," Jewel looked at him. "Did you?" Rory asked. "I was too busy staring at you when you were talking. I didn't register a thing."

"So why is this so fascinating today?" Jewel asked.

"I was just looking for Octavia," Rory said. "My mom said something this morning about Octavia and Mercedes. I wanted to see her picture."

"I don't have a picture of her," Jewel said. "I didn't know about her until Lester mentioned that I looked like her. Then he said she died in a horrible car crash along with her ex-husband. That's why he inherited that house he showed off the other day. He was her next of kin."

"I want to see her picture," Rory said.

"According to Lester, you just need to look at me," Jewel joked. "Wait a minute...is that why your mother doesn't like me?"

"I think so. Maybe it's one of the reasons," Rory said. "She had an affair with Lester, not knowing he was married and had Jeremiah. You're related to Lester."

"But so is Jeremiah, and she likes him just fine," Jewel said. "What did she say about Octavia?"

"Nothing. They clammed up when I asked," Rory frowned. "What do you know about her?"

"She died in a car crash. She was close to Lester. Her husband was a doctor. They were in the middle of a divorce," Jewel said.

"What kind of doctor was he?" Rory frowned.

"What does it matter?" Jewel asked.

"I don't know. There are whispers in the family that Aunt Claudia wasn't all there," Rory pointed to his head.

"Ah, I see," Jewel nodded. "Is it something she inherited?"

"I don't think so," Rory said. "Out of my mother's eleven siblings, she's the only one that had it. They don't like talking about her, partly because of Mercedes. They don't want to say anything bad about her biological mother, and partly because they don't like dwelling on the negatives of life, you know?

"Aunt Claudia died in childbirth. My mother was the sibling they called when she had the baby. She and Dad officially adopted Mercedes. That's all I know," Rory said.

"Maybe that's all we should know. People have their secrets," Jewel shrugged. "Let's forget about it and have a good time at the party. I'm looking forward to all the nice things to eat. I'm starving."

****

The Christmas holidays were winding down, and Rory was to return to school tomorrow. He was sitting in the home office across from his mother's desk. She had requested that he join her to discuss his finances for the upcoming semester. She hadn't yet taken off her power suit from work. She looked solemn and slightly combative, as if they were competitors at war. He didn't know what he had done to deserve this approach.

Perhaps it was the fact that he had stayed out late last night, hanging with Jewel at her place. He had spent the whole of New Year's Day with her and her mother, Pearl. It was fun. Pearl was hilarious and an excellent cook, something she said she didn't get to do enough of.

He knew his mother was going to be upset with him. He had tried to avoid her when she was leaving for work, only to be summoned to a meeting with her after work.

He had never had a financial meeting with Bunny before. His parents took care of his bills, gave him a credit card, and money appeared in his account monthly without him having to ask.

He usually budgeted that money wisely, sometimes not using it at all.

"Before you go back to school," Bunny said thoughtfully, "I want you to do something for me."

"What?" Rory asked curiously.

"I want you to phase that girl Jewel out of your life."

"Why should I?" Rory asked, exasperated.

He hated how his mother had been acting since the Christmas party. Jewel had been a hit with the family.

Everybody liked her, except for Bunny.

It was strange. He thought his mother would have warmed up to her by now, but Bunny used every excuse in the book to find fault with her.

"If you don't break up with her," Bunny said, "I will cut your allowance."

Rory looked at her in disbelief. "Why would you do that?"

"I will take back your credit cards, take back your car, and not pay your school fee for next year or while you are at college."

"You can't be serious!" Rory whistled. "What's going on, Mom?"

"I cannot stand her," Bunny said. "I tried to like her, but I can't. It's not happening. I want her as far away from this family as possible. I am sorry, but that's the way I feel."

"I see," Rory said heavily.

"I won't lodge your allowance until you say you will do it," Bunny said, her expression determined.

Rory inhaled. He had money apart from his allowance, which his parents had set up for all their children, but it was in a secure savings account that he couldn't touch until he was twenty-one. He also saved his earnings diligently since he was twelve from all the jobs his father would have them on, but that was in an investment account he had co-signed with his mother because he needed an adult's signature. Somehow, he didn't feel as if she would help him get that money.

If he wanted to keep seeing Jewel, he would have to lie to his mother and do it secretly. The thought didn't sit well in his brain. He hated lying, especially to her. But why was she being so unreasonable? Her behavior was not normal.

"I could tell you I'm not going to see her anymore just so that I can get my allowance and get an education," Rory pointed out calmly. He didn't know why he was so calm; he felt like shouting at the injustice of it all. Why couldn't he see Jewel if he wanted to? What type of dictatorship was his once mild-mannered mother on?

"Oh no, I won't take your word for it," Bunny clasped her hands in front of her and looked at him like she would a competitor. Where was his loving mother behind this cold woman sitting in the chair at her home office, treating him like a stranger?

"I will watch you to make sure you do it."

"You're going to hire a detective to spy on me?" Rory asked incredulously.

"That I will do," Bunny said, her hands hovering over her checkbook. "What will it be, Rory?"

"I promised her I would drop her off at school. She doesn't have a vehicle."

"And that's fine. You can say your goodbyes then," Bunny scribbled on the checkbook. "This is post-dated for the day after tomorrow. If you don't break it off, that check will bounce."

"Rory swallowed, "Yes, ma'am."

"And don't bother appealing to your father," Bunny said. "He told me to handle this any way I see fit, so I'm handling it the way I want to."

"Exactly what are you handling?" Rory got up. "I don't understand this. You used to tell me that I could talk to you about anything. Why can't you talk to me about this instead of acting like a beast?"

Bunny looked at him pleadingly. "You can talk to me about anything."

"No," Rory shook his head. "This whole thing with Jewel has changed us. I never thought I would see the day when I found out I didn't like you as a person, Mom."

Bunny blinked rapidly. "With time, you will forget her, and then you'll move on. This is for the best."

Chapter Nine

It was a long car ride to the university. Jewel could tell that something was going on with Rory. He was troubled about something. He wasn't saying what it was. Though she had known him for a short time she knew him well enough to figure out that he was troubled.

"You can tell me what it is, you know?" Jewel said after two songs had finished playing and they hadn't said anything to each other.

"My mother doesn't want me to have a relationship with you," Rory glanced at her. "She is threatening to stop paying my school fee and snatch my allowance unless I stop seeing you."

"Oh wow," Jewel widened her eyes. "What is it about me that triggers her that much?"

"I don't know," Rory sighed heavily.

"We could pretend that we are not seeing each other," Jewel offered.

"It won't work. She is going to hire someone to spy on me," Rory muttered. "There has to be a clean break."

Jewel nodded. Her heart was breaking. She really liked Rory, and the Christmas holidays had only cemented that.

"You know what," she said out loud, "it's okay. There is no reason to get messed up over this. We'll just be friends; we'll say hi and bye if we see each other in the hallways. I wouldn't want you to lose your education over this, and your mother sounds pretty determined that we part ways."

Rory looked at her thoughtfully and then back on the road. "Are you sure that's okay for you?"

"It's fine," Jewel said flippantly. "It's the first year of university. It's bound to happen. We'll meet people and have friends; we will lose those same people along the way. That's just the way of life."

Rory sighed.

He felt uneasy about it. He didn't want to lose her, but he hadn't thought of a way to circumvent his mother's ridiculous demands. He hadn't even told any of his siblings yet. It had been so sudden and unexpected. Bunny had blindsided him with her demands. He hadn't even asked his father if he agreed with what was happening.

What would his dad do anyway? Bobby rarely intervened with Bunny's decisions when it came to them.

He couldn't help but feel bullied into walking away from Jewel. There was a tight knot at the pit of his stomach.

"So, I'll see you around," Jewel said when they reached her door. She even held out her hand for a handshake.

As Rory solemnly shook her hand, he quietly contemplated choosing her over his time at university and calling his mother's bluff. Surely, she wouldn't make him quit school over Jewel.

"Don't think so hard," Jewel reached up and kissed him

on his cheek. "It will work out; however, it is supposed to work out."

Rory nodded and stepped back. "See you around."

"See you around," Jewel said huskily as she closed the door on his woebegone face and inhaled and exhaled rapidly.

When the tears came, they came slowly and then rapidly. She ran into her room, lay on the bed, covered her head with a pillow, and howled. Bunny Nelson thought something was wrong with her.

It was hard to accept when someone thought you were not good enough for their son. The more she thought about it, the angrier she became.

She stopped crying long enough to call Pearl and then cried some more when Pearl answered the phone. Pearl was not exactly understanding.

"You'll find someone else," she said soothingly. "It's your first break up; life goes on." "Thanks a lot, Pearl," Jewel muttered when she hung up the phone.

She wasn't going to mope around the place because she had broken up with Rory. No way, no how. She was going to live her life like he was never in it.

****

January made way for February. Jewel saw Rory around campus and even saw him in the hallway once. He helped her with her groceries, and she smiled and thanked him.

"How's it going?" Rory asked.

"Good," Jewel said.

And then Kenny told her they were going to a pre-Valentine concert. That was when she snapped and went out with Ray Conrad. He had not stopped sending her gifts every week like clockwork, and she hadn't dismissed him totally from her life; she just had not given him any encouragement.

Their date was a disaster. He was too touchy-feely for her taste, and they shared a sloppy kiss that had her washing out her mouth with mouthwash when she got home. Unfortunately, that kiss was witnessed by Rory, Audra, and Kenny in the apartment parking lot when she had finally pulled herself out of Ray's arms.

She saw the expression of disgust and devastation on Rory's face, and she wondered why she still cared. Her first thought was, 'good, let him suffer. This was what you got. You decided to ditch me because of your mother'. But then, her second thought was not quite as diabolical.

She missed him. She missed them. And then it dawned on her. She loved Rory. He was her person.

****

"**Y**ou made your mom make you give up, Jewel. You are stupid," Camden said. "And look at you now. Lonely for spring break."

"Will you shut up?" Rory growled. "Nobody asked for your opinion."

"I would never give up that girl for anything," Camden said. "If she were mine, I'd lick her dirty boots."

"Get out of my room!"

"I'm going. Some people get one chance with a hot girl. You got yours, and you blew it. Or maybe she wasn't so into you as you thought," Camden chuckled. "You lost your chance. She's now with her big architect."

Rory winced. "He was still recovering from seeing Jewel kissing that guy. Was she sleeping with him? How much of a couple were they?

It was killing him inside.

"There was no joy in his life anymore, he was so down and out."

He called his parents and told them he was not coming home for the midterm break.

"Why not?" Bunny asked. "You're not still seeing that girl, are you?"

"No," Rory said.

"Good," Bunny said. "You've always been obedient."

When he hung up from his mother, he felt empty.

He was distressed and disloyal. He felt like a man torn in two directions. One direction was the dutiful son, and the other was a man who had not managed to shake his love for Jewel.

He was distressed enough to call Mercedes. Was she in the process of doing her master's degree in counselling or was it psychotherapy? He didn't remember. He just knew that he needed her counsel. She always gave good counsel anyway.

"I broke up with Jewel because of Mom," he said after Mercedes greeted him, and he explained why he wasn't coming home.

"That is not a normal request for mom to make," Mercedes said, shocked.

"I know," Rory said, feeling vindicated that he was not the only one who found their mother's Gestapo-like demand abnormal.

"I didn't want to do it; I should have called her bluff. Do you really think she would stop me from going to school because she opposes Jewel?"

"It depends on how determined she is," Mercedes said, "and there is always dad to appeal to. He could rein her in. He is normally the calmer of the two of them when it comes to domestic disputes like these."

"I've never been disobedient before," Rory looked up at the ceiling. "I was seriously contemplating being disobedient then. What would you do if you were me?"

Mercedes cleared her throat. "Goodness, I don't think I should answer that based on how rebellious I can get. I am just a smidge better than Larry when defying authority. I just hide it better."

"Come on," Rory said, "tell me what you would do."

"Well," Mercedes said, "how do you feel about her?"

"I love her," Rory said. "I saw her kissing someone else today, and my heart constricted. I couldn't breathe for a second. She's all I have been thinking about this semester, I might fail all my courses, and I haven't gotten my head in the game this year. What I have for her is not a fleeting crush on a pretty girl. I think we really gel. I can't explain it. Maybe it's a cliché, but I think she's the one. She'll always be the one."

"Mmm," Mercedes murmured. "If I were to feel that way about a guy, which, for the record, I have never felt, I would, first of all, be thankful for the miracle."

Rory chuckled.

"And if he feels the same way about me, I would marry him," Mercedes said. "Marriage is a done deal. Mom would have no say about me seeing him again because, obviously, I would have shut it all down and taken the wind out of her sail."

Rory sat up in bed. "Marriage? Don't you think that is a bit extreme?"

"Nope," Mercedes said. "I think that's the only way that mom will accept your relationship. Dad would not allow you to be a married man without having the means to provide for your new family, so the threats about your allowance would stop. Knowing Dad, you would get more. You two could find a small apartment near campus and live together. If you can survive that, then it will be worth it. Mom would not have a leg to stand on."

"Wow," Rory whistled. "You are a genius, thank you."

"Don't thank me yet," Mercedes warned. "Jewel may laugh in your face when you propose."

"There is that," Rory said, deflated again.

"As well as she might not," Mercedes continued. "By the way, if anybody asks why you are married at eighteen, in your first year of college, don't mention me, please. However, I want credit if your marriage can stand the test of time."

Rory chuckled. "Thanks, Mercedes; you are my favorite sister for a reason."

"I am your only sister, knucklehead," Mercedes said. "Tell me how it goes."

After he hung up the phone from Mercedes, Rory contemplated how he would propose to Jewel.

****

"I am going to propose to Jewel on Valentine's Day," Rory announced to his friends. They were visiting Audra, who was in the hospital with a broken wrist and a neck brace after falling down a flight of stairs the day before.

"I think my ears are broken too," Audra said mournfully. "I just heard propose. Maybe you should get my doctor; my hearing has gone wonky."

"Your hearing is not wonky. I heard it too," Kenny looked at Rory incredulously. "You did say propose, didn't you?"

"He said it," Camden shook his head. "And I think it's this place; some psychedelic drug must be wafting in the air, messing with his brain."

"My sister suggested it, and the more I think about it, the more I realize it's not a bad suggestion. Why couldn't we make a marriage work?"

"Because you barely know her," Kenny said.

"You two would make pretty babies together," Audra said dreamily. "I love babies."

"They gave you too much morphine," Camden patted Audra's foot sympathetically. "Rory is joking with us."

"I am not," Rory said. "I am going to do it."

"You do know that she sees someone else?" Camden said. "We saw her kissing him the other night."

Rory nodded. "I saw it. It's burned behind my eyes. And it still leaves a bad taste in my mouth."

"You are too young to get married," Camden said. "Have a normal relationship first, date around, and then, if she's the one, get married when you are forty."

"That's bad advice," Kenny said. "If she's the one, why date around and get into all sorts of relationship turmoil before you commit. All you have to do is work at it like any other long-term relationship."

"My concern is that you have only known her for a couple of weeks," Kenny said. "You had a nice time together at Christmas, and then you broke up, and now you want to marry her to get your mother off your back. In my humble opinion, that is not a good reason to get married."

"I second that," Audra said. "Get to know her for a while first."

"Okay, I'll propose to her over the Easter holidays. We'll get married in the summer," Rory said.

"Kenny chuckled, "I was thinking more like a year or two, not a month or two."

"It's not going to work," Camden said balefully. "She won't say yes."

"I am happy to see you are happy for me," Rory said sarcastically.

"Just don't put your expectations too high," Camden

warned. "Maybe she doesn't feel the same way about you."

****

Valentine's Day on a university campus was the same as high school, Jewel thought absently. There were the usual happy and in-love couples who exchanged gifts and had no qualms walking around with their flowers, chocolates, and teddy bears to stick it to the single people who had no gifts.

And then there were some single people who couldn't stand to be left out, who bought their own gifts to fit in. Then there were the "Palentines" people who exchanged presents and hung out together as friends to counteract the so-called lover's day.

And then there were people like her, who had scores of admirers, several invitations to various events, and too many presents to count. She just wanted the day to end. The person she wanted to be her valentine had to stay away from her because of his mother. The irony was not lost on her; she was spoiled for choice, but the one she wanted was unavailable.

She felt like accosting Rory and demanding that he choose her over his mother and education, but she wouldn't do it, of course. It was just a selfish thought that she had contemplated throughout the day.

What was for sure, she wasn't going to try and replace him with anyone again. The Ray Conrad date had been such a disaster, she had told him that she wasn't interested in him. Going out with him had been a monumental mistake. She hadn't even tried to spare the poor man's feelings.

"You walk fast," Kenny said, panting behind her. "I saw you leaving the building, and I had to make a mad dash to try and catch you."

"Sorry," Jewel looked at her. "I was thinking. When I

think, I walk fast. What's up?"

Any news on Rory? Jewel wanted to ask. Like, who is his Valentine? Is she Bunny-approved? But she didn't.

Kenny had somehow managed to compartmentalize her friendship with Rory from her friendship with Jewel. She didn't mention him if she didn't have to, and Jewel was not going to sound needy and ask about him when Rory had probably moved on.

"I know you're probably going somewhere exotic and romantic with one of your admirers later," Kenny said. "But we're having a Palentines Party, and I just had to invite you, just in case."

"I'm not going anywhere," Jewel sighed. "And I'm not in the mood to party. Thank you for the invite, though."

"Strange," Kenny smirked. "That's the same response I got from Rory. The two of you are really taking this being away from each other hard, aren't you?"

"He's taking it hard?" Jewel asked breathlessly.

"Oh yes," Kenny continued. "Probably failing all his courses, and he's been psyching himself up to prop..."

"Prop?" Jewel stopped walking. "What's prop?"

"Propagate, propel. Yes, propel himself over to your place," Kenny said weakly.

Jewel looked at her suspiciously. "What aren't you telling me?"

"Nothing," Kenny said breezily. "Just in case you change your mind about the party, though, it's at Liam's cottage, you know the one."

She walked away hurriedly. Jewel couldn't help the smile that crept along her face. Suddenly, it wasn't such a bad Valentine's Day after all. Maybe she should "accidentally on purpose" run into Rory at their building, and maybe she should be dressed up to the nines, let him see what he was missing.

****

Rory stood nervously at Jewel's door. It was way after six. He knew she was home; he had seen her walking jauntily in the parking lot, looking almost as happy as when she had seen the pastry table at the Christmas table.

What had she been so happy about? And was he in for an embarrassing slam of the door in his face?

He dithered before the door. Uncertainty didn't begin to describe him. He swallowed several times before knocking and then shoved his trembling fingers in his pockets, where it hit on the ring box. He had used most of his allowance to buy the ring.

Jewel pulled the door open. She was dressed in a red and black baby doll dress with a little bow at the front. Her hair was out and about her shoulders in ringlets, and she smelled divine.

"I didn't know you were going out," Rory stammered.

"I am not," Jewel said. "Just felt like dressing up for Valentine's Day. Come on in."

Rory stepped inside the apartment door and closed it, leaning on it for strength. His heart was pounding in his chest. He had spent several sleepless nights wondering how this scenario would go, and now that the moment was here, words failed him.

"Rory?" Jewel smiled at him slightly. "What's wrong? You look terrified."

"I have to ask you something," Rory said.

Jewel nodded. "Okay, so ask."

"My mother has made it clear that she disapproves of us, but I can't help how I feel about you. I love you, Jewel. I probably fell in love with you from the first moment I saw you, and I can't imagine my life without you. These last couple of weeks have been tough. I would..."

Tears welled up in Jewel's eyes as she listened to Rory.

"Go on," she whispered.

"How do you feel about me?" Rory asked uncertainly. "I saw you kissing Conrad."

"He kissed me," Jewel made a face. "That will never happen again. I told him I wasn't interested."

Rory sighed in relief.

"Rory, I love you too," Jewel said, her voice choking with emotion. "But are you sure this is what you want? Are you sure you're ready to go against your mother for me? What about your education and her having you watched?"

Rory's eyes met hers, filled with determination. "I think we should get married. She can't trouble us then. It will be a done deal."

"Married?" Jewel squealed. "As in wedding? As in, till death do us part?"

Rory nodded.

"I need to sit down," Jewel walked to the sofa and sat down hard.

Rory sat beside her. "I know this is sudden and a big ask, but..."

"Yes, I will marry you, Rory," Jewel whispered, looking at him. "I might be out of my mind, but I feel as if the two of us will work together for a long, long time."

Rory's smile lit up his face.

He took the ring box out of his pocket and opened it. "We'll face our obstacles together," Rory said, sliding the ring on her finger. "We'll defy anyone or anything that stands in the way of our love."

Chapter Ten

They got married at the chapel on campus, and Jewel wore a white dress she had bought on a sale downtown.

Rory wore his best church suit.

They had a small guest list. On Rory's side were Kenny, Camden, and Audra; they were in various states of incredulity that it was really happening. His siblings Jeremiah and Mercedes were there and sworn to secrecy. Larry couldn't make it. He didn't get any time off for the summer. He, too, was told not to say a word to Bunny and Bobby.

Jewel invited her cousin Lester and his wife Kristine, who insisted on paying for her honeymoon, and Pearl, who was skeptical about her choosing Rory over the architect.

"I guess you'll grow together," Pearl said. "He's from a good family. When I said get married to a rich man, I was thinking of an established man who had his own thing going on, not a boy.

"Are you coming to the wedding? Yes, or no?" Jewel

asked.

"Of course," Pearl said. "You are my only child. And even if you weren't, I would still be there. I know Rory's mom will be pissed that he didn't tell her. You said his family was close?"

"Yes, they are," Jewel said. "But his mother practically forbid him to see me, so we decided not to invite her or his dad in order not to create friction."

"And what if they disown him?" Pearl asked worriedly.

Jewel laughed. "Then we work together and build our future independently from them."

"I was afraid of this," Pearl grumbled. "You got bitten by the love bug, didn't you?"

"I did," Jewel giggled.

"Marriage is such a big step, Jew," Pearl said.

"It wasn't a big step when you thought I was going to marry a rich man, though," Jewel said.

"That's right," Pearl said. "And I have no apologies for that. Women need to aim high in this economic environment, but I will concede that there is room for growth together and that I can get behind. Speaking of growth, I don't want to hijack your good news."

"Talk to me," Jewel urged.

"I might be getting a new job," Pearl said with anticipation. "I have been putting my feelers out there."

"And what if Leonard discovers this?" Jewel asked. "Your life could be in danger."

"I have been asking discreetly," Pearl said. "Remember my producer, buddy? He's well connected."

"Oh yes, that guy," Jewel said. "How is it going with him?"

"Oh, Chex Hastings," Pearl said. "I wasn't really into him. He's nice, rich, handsome, and all of that, but we didn't kick it off. I see myself getting married and having children in the future. I can't see myself doing that with him. He is the type of guy you have a couple of months with, and then he is on to the next, you know what I mean?"

"So, it's not all about the money after all," Jewel murmured.

"I guess not," Pearl said. "And that is why I am not even knocking what you have with Rory. If there is a slim chance that you can eke out a happy ending in this life, I am all for it. You know what Mama said before Norman died?"

"No," Jewel murmured.

"She said she wished she had met him sooner so they could have had a longer time together. In their case, they only got five years. You have a lifetime of potential with Rory; cherish it."

****

Jewel walked up the aisle in the off-the-rack white dress that fit her like it was custom-made. She had styled her hair in soft curls parted to one side, and a white flower fascinator jauntily covered one eye. A red rose bouquet completed her bridal look.

She felt at peace. That was the only way to describe it as Lester escorted her toward Rory.

He made for a dashing groom in his formal suit. It was the first time she was seeing him decked out in formal wear.

He looked handsome, debonair, and polished.

When she approached him, their eyes locked. Her heart skipped a beat. He smiled and took her hand in his, holding her firmly and reassuringly.

"You look beautiful," Rory murmured. "I am a lucky man."

As they stood together before the altar, they exchanged their vows.

Jewel said, "Rory, you are my best friend, partner, and everything. I promise to love and support you through life's ups and downs. I can't wait to spend forever with you."

Rory responded, "My dearest Jewel, you have changed my life in every way imaginable. You are my everything, my reason for living. I promise to love, honor, and cherish you for all the days of my life. I can't wait to spend forever with you."

They had an impromptu reception organized by Audra and thrown for them at Biscuits, the same restaurant where they first saw each other. It was tastefully decorated in red and white; the food was extra tasty, and though the size of the crowd was small, they were having a whale of a time.

"I would like to propose a toast as best man," Camden said, standing up. "Rory and I have known each other since we were little kids, and I am honored to stand here as his best man today. I couldn't be happier for him to have found his soulmate in Jewel. You deserve all the happiness in the world, Rory. I know you and Jewel will have a lifetime of love and happiness together. So, let us all raise our glasses and toast to the happy couple, Rory and Jewel. Cheers!"

"That was sweet of Camden," Kenny said. "I am the maid of honor and a friend to both the bride and groom. I've known Jewel for a couple of months, and from what I know, I love her. I think she and Rory will make the long haul.

"My parents married after high school and were together until my dad's death twenty years later. My mom said people asked how they stayed together for so long, and she said they both considered each other home. As a soon-to-be architect, I think this is appropriate advice for you, Rory. Consider Jewel your place, your home. And Jewel, consider him your place. You both know that nothing in life is smooth sailing, but if there is a safe place in the storm, you should be able to find that place in each other."

"Oh wow," Jewel whispered. "That is totally deep."

"I know," Rory said contemplatively. "When did Kenny become so wise?"

Kenny chuckled. "Just look at each other deep in the eyes and tell each other there is no place like you."

"No place like you, Rory," Jewel said, "and I mean it."

"No place like you, Jewel," Rory reached over and kissed her.

****

Lester's gift to them for their honeymoon was a week's stay at a private villa in the Blue Mountains.

"Oh wow," Jewel said. "This is the best gift ever. It's as if you can walk out on a cloud." They were standing on the balcony. Rory wrapped his arms around her. "It is a lovely gift. We cannot, for any reason, tell my mother about this."

"Your secret is safe with me," Jewel said. "All your secrets."

"We'll have to live with her this summer," Rory said.

"We'll worry about that when we come to it," Jewel said. "But right now, I'm married to you. I feel so free and in love and totally safe with you."

Rory gently ran his fingers through Jewel's hair, and she closed her eyes, savoring the moment. He leaned in to kiss her, and she responded with a passionate kiss of her own. They undressed each other, revealing their bodies to each other for the first time. The sight of each other's bare skin sent shivers down their spines. They explored each other's bodies, learning what made the other person feel good.

As they made love, they felt a deep connection, like they were truly one. It was a moment they would never forget. Afterward, as they lay in each other's arms, they knew they were meant to be together forever. They had found true love and couldn't wait to spend the rest of their lives exploring it.

Chapter Eleven

It was the hardest conversation he had ever had.

Rory told his father first to lessen the blow.

"Dad, can you tell Mom for me?" Rory asked.

"No, son," Bobby laughed. "You're a married man now. Congratulations to you and Jewel. You have my unwavering support, and you'll always have it. Let me go and get your mother."

"Hello, honey?" Bunny said when she came on the phone, quite oblivious to what he was about to tell her next.

"I thought you should know before I come home that I got married to Jewel a month ago, and when I come home this summer, it will be the two of us. I was thinking we should stay in the apartment above the garage until I finish my house. It would be out of your hair, and we wouldn't need to bother you much."

Bunny didn't say a word, he only heard sobs, loud sobs.

Bobby came back on the phone. "You said something

about the garage?"

"Yes," Rory said glumly. "We hardly use that space, and it has a separate entrance."

"Yes, it would be perfect," Bobby said, "that's where Bunny and I lived when we just got married while we worked on the main house. It needs work and some modernizing." I'll have Larry renovate it for you and Jewel. It's not a bad place to start out."

His father really knew how to put him at ease.

"Thanks, Dad," Rory said gratefully. "I almost thought I wouldn't have anywhere to go."

"Ridiculous." Bobby snorted, "you are my son. I love you unconditionally. You will always have a home here. I will never reject you. I don't think there is anything you or Jeremiah, Larry, or Mercedes can do to make me turn my back on any of you. Nothing, or no one, can do that."

"Thanks, Dad," Rory said.

"Your mother feels the same, too," Bobby said, "she has her issues with Jewel's family, which I hope she will one day share, but you must know that you didn't have to marry Jewel to be with her. Your mother was bluffing about school and your allowance. Even if she wasn't, there is no way on earth I would have allowed your mother to leave you broke and without an education."

"She seemed serious at the time," Rory said.

"She had to appear to be serious." Bobby sighed, "and in her efforts to keep you away from Jewel, she only brought you closer. I knew it would happen."

"I love Jewel. I think we would have ended up here anyway." Rory said, "we'd either be living together or something. I don't want to be without her."

"I understand," Bobby said, "what's done is done. We'll have to talk about your allowance, where you will live next year at college, and all of that stuff, but when you get home and your mother is a bit more coherent, we'll sit down and work it out. This will teach her about bullying her children into doing her bidding; it never works out the way you want it to."

Rory heard his mother sobbing even louder.

"Looking forward to having you and Jewel home, son," Bobby said.

****

His mother was conspicuously absent when he arrived home with Jewel. Larry was the one that met them in the front yard by the garage.

"Ahoy there, brother and new sister-in-law!" Larry hugged him first and then Jewel. "Sorry I couldn't make it to the wedding. I have made it up to you both by designing the luxury two-bedroom, two-bath apartment of your dreams. Dad said I should spare no expense, and I think I went hog wild."

Jewel clapped her hands, "I can't wait!"

"Right this way," Larry said, grinning. "There's an alcove with a door beside the three-car garage. The door has an intercom, and I put in a camera," he pointed at the camera.

"Cool," Rory nodded.

"The areca palms were Mercedes' idea," Larry said, pointing to the two potted palms on the landing. "Please don't kill them, Rory and Jewel."

"We won't," Jewel said. "I love plants."

"Good. All you need to do is change the water at the bottom every two months or so," Larry said. "These are self-watering pots."

"Nice," Rory said. "Then they definitely won't be killed."

They headed up a flight of stairs and into an open-plan living room and kitchen, with balcony doors opening up to a patio. It was fully furnished in neutral grey tones with green accents.

"Oh, my word!" Jewel gasped. "It's gorgeous! I love the color scheme, grey, green, black, and white!"

"I remembered," Larry said, "from when we were doing that charity project. You kept saying that grey and green were a match made in heaven. So here you are, neutral shades of grey with varying shades of green as accents, and of course, the basic neutrals black and white."

"It is chic and relaxing at the same time," Rory looked around. "I am rating this a ten out of ten, Larry."

Jewel headed for the balcony, opening the doors and inhaling deeply. "I can see the ocean from here!"

Rory smiled. "I guess I made the right call asking Dad for this place."

"You should have seen it before," Larry said. "It took several trips to the dumpster to clean it out. They really were using it for junk for all these years. I couldn't believe it was so nice when I saw it. I wish I had thought of it when I was younger, but I probably wouldn't have been motivated to build my own place. Don't get too comfortable up here, Rory. You still need to do your own."

Rory nodded. "When I graduate, I will do it."

He walked over to the first bedroom; it already had all his things from his old room.

"That's a new bed brend side tables and paintings," Larry said, "Mom said I shouldn't leave your old room completely bare. She still goes in there and cry, clutching your old teddy bear, wishing things were different between you two."

Rory laughed. "Mom is too busy at the office and has no time for that. And I never had any teddy bears. You are hilarious."

Larry shrugged. "She has been a little under the weather about the estrangement between you two."

"The estrangement is not my doing; I will not take the blame for any of it," Rory said, "Thank you for moving my stuff."

"You have Mercedes and Jeremiah to thank for that," Larry said. "I just directed them."

"Oh, my word, the paintings," Jewel returned to the living room. "They are glorious." "Those are courtesy of Mercedes," Larry said. "She bought them from a gallery. She said that paintings seemed like a better fit than pictures up here. I would agree with her."

Jewel stood back and looked at the abstract painting in greens and greys. "It's pulling me in. There is something compelling about it."

"I didn't know you were an art connoisseur," Rory said, standing beside her. "I see what you mean. It's chaotic and peaceful at the same time. I wonder how the artist managed to do all that in an abstract?"

He went closer to the painting. "Orandy Dennis. Who is Orandy Dennis"

"That's Lee, and Derrick's brother," Larry said. "He is an artist."

"He's good," Jewel said.

"That's what Mercedes said," Larry nodded. "There is another piece from him. It's in the master bedroom. I'll leave you two to it. I hope you will be happy here."

"Oh, before I forget," Larry said. "Shay said you are to give her a call, Jewel. There is an open slot for one more summer worker at her workplace."

Jewel squealed. "Thank God! I haven't heard back from a single business that I sent my resume. I'll call her now. I want that slot. Thanks, Larry. Seriously, thank you."

"No problem," Larry said. "Oh, and another thing. Mom is inviting you two to dinner."

"Good God, do I have to go?" Jewel asked.

"At least go once," Rory said. "It may not be that bad."

****

It was bad. Jewel thought with trepidation. It was her first time seeing Bunny since the hostility of the Christmas holiday when she had forbidden Rory to see her.

She had since married her son, against her wishes, and hadn't invited her to the wedding. Of course, nobody was expecting an easy time of it. That may have been why Mercedes, ever the buffer and peacemaker, was there to greet them at the patio door.

"I know my mother," Mercedes whispered to Jewel. "She will not respect you if you take her insults and whimper like a doormat. Give it back to her as good as you get it."

"You mean insult her back?" Jewel asked. "I don't practice being rude to people, and I don't want to be rude to Bunny."

"That's right, her name is Bunny," Mercedes said. "Everybody calls her Bunny. Don't let her pigeonhole you into calling her Mrs. Nelson. It's ridiculous. If you call her Mrs. Nelson, you'll have to call my dad Mr. Nelson. He's quite fine with plain old Bobby, especially from friends and family."

Jewel nodded.

"Next thing, she'll become passive-aggressive and try to make you cry and run away from the table. Harden your resolve not to do it. The minute she latches on to that weakness, you'll be toast."

Jewel frowned. "This feels like war."

"It is," Mercedes said. "Do not show weakness or fear. Give as good as you get."

"Thank you," Jewel said. "I am grateful to you guys for accepting me, despite Bunny's dislike."

"I inexplicably like you," Mercedes hugged her. "I am usually very accurate in assessing people. You are a good person, and I am happy that you love my brother."

Bunny sailed into the dining room with a tight smile on her face.

Bobby walked behind her. "Good evening, everyone."

"Hey, Dad," Mercedes, Jeremiah, and Rory greeted him.

"Hello, Bobby," Jewel said. It felt strange to call him that. She had "Mr. Nelson-ed" him over Christmas, only to discover that he hated it.

"Well, we are all together now," Bunny said. "I must confess that these past weeks have been somewhat hard for me, as everyone knows my baby, Rory, got married without telling me. Apparently, everyone else in this family knew except for me."

Rory sighed. "Mom..."

"There is no excuse," Bunny said, her eyes watering. "I was the last to know. I heard a month after! A month! I am not going to pretend that it doesn't hurt."

She sniffed. "I will acknowledge that my behavior until then was inexcusable. I told you to leave Jewel. I threatened your allowance and your school fees. I am sorry. I went too far, and I was wrong."

"Oh, Mom," Rory got up and hugged his mother. "You are forgiven. I just want to understand why you are doing this."

They hugged for a long while until Bunny stepped away. "I don't want to get into that now. I must say, though, that I can't pretend that I have suddenly changed and that I like you, Jewel," Bunny said, looking at her. "But whether I like it or not, you are now family, and the Nelson family excels at sticking together. I will grudgingly welcome you to the family and hope that maybe one day there is no grudge there."

Jewel nodded. "Well, thank you for the begrudging welcome, Bunny. I will be just as grateful for an unbegrudging welcome as well."

Bunny widened her eyes and then narrowed them. "So, the cat has claws."

"I have never thought of myself as a cat," Jewel mused. "But I have always appreciated that felines are beautiful animals."

"Goodness," Mercedes laughed. "This is good!"

"Oh, shut up, Mercedes," Bunny grunted. "I see your hands all over this."

Mercedes smiled innocently. "Whatever do you mean, mother?"

Bunny grunted and looked at Jewel. "I hope you like curried goat. This is my pathetic attempt at a reception feast. I even had Jill bake a cake."

"I love curried goat," Jewel said.

"Well, as my husband likes to say," Bunny said, "what's done is done. We will both try to move on."

"I'd like that," Jewel sighed in relief.

The tension slowly dissipated, and the Nelson family continued their dinner-time ritual.

Chapter Twelve

Present day, two years later

"First day of work for both of us tomorrow." Jewel ruffled in her Jewelry box for a pair of earrings. It was Larry's and Jill's wedding day. The theme was blue and white, so she was dressed in a baby blue dress, as requested by Jill for the family photos.

Rory came behind her as soon as she found the diamond studs. "You look awesome," he said. "You don't look bad yourself, Mr. Nelson," Jewel said, smiling at him in the mirror.

Rory was dressed in a navy-blue vest because he was one of the groomsmen.

He hugged her from behind. "You aren't jealous, are you, that they're having a big wedding and everything?"

"Not in the least. I loved my wedding," Jewel smiled. "Are you jealous?"

"No," Rory kissed her on the neck. "I'm happy for them. I

love to see my brothers happy."

"Me too," Jill said. "I'm sure your mother will point out for the thousandth time that she got to attend all her son's weddings except yours."

"That may be the only thing I regret at this point. Two years later, and my mom cannot let go the bee she has in her bonnet." Rory said, "I thought you two would have started to get along by now."

"I don't know about that," Jewel said. "Bunny may never forgive me for marrying her baby and thwarting her plans to keep us apart."

She looked at him appreciatively. Even though Rory looked nothing like a baby, he had outgrown the boyish cuteness. He was full-fledged handsome, and manly.

"Don't look at me like that," Rory whispered. "We'll be late. I'll mess up your hair."

Jewel grinned. "How am I looking at you, Rory?

"Like I'm one of Jill's cakes, and you want to devour me in one bite."

Jewel laughed. "Speaking of Jill, I can't believe she's going to be our neighbor. And my sister-in-law. I wonder if she is moving her cats with her?"

"No, I heard that she is letting them stay where they are." Rory said, "She is at the bakery in the days anyway."

Her phone rang. Jewel groaned. "That must be Kenny. She has been calling me every hour on the hour because she starts tomorrow too, and she's too excited to process it."

Rory grinned. "Want me to answer?"

"Yup. Tell her we are running late for the wedding, and I can't find my shoes. Where are those shoes?"

Rory answered the phone, spoke to Kenny, and then watched her indulgently as she frantically searched from one room to another.

"Say, Jewel, are you looking for the shoes that match your dress?"

"Yes!" Jewel said, pausing at the guest room door.

"They are by the stairs!" Rory said. "Come on, let's go. I don't want to be late for the pre-wedding gathering of the groomsmen."

****

Jewel knew that the wedding would be spectacular. Jill was popular, she had a huge family, and so did Larry.

Jewel arrived at the church a little before the wedding started. The Nelson side of the aisle was almost full. An usher, probably one of Jill's church sisters, took her to the very front of the church, where she was seated beside Bunny.

Jewel groaned inwardly, her motto through the years was to avoid Bunny at all cost.

"Sorry, I can't be a buffer," Shay said. "I have the baby, and I have to be in the aisle seat so I can disappear whenever this little one starts crying."

Jewel looked over at Anjou Nelson and smiled. He looked more like a miniature Webb than his sister Cerise did. While Cerise was a miniature Bunny, Anjou was all Webb. He looked just like Lester and, by extension her. She had taken a picture with Anjou and put it on one of her social media accounts. People were telling her congratulations; her son looked like her.

Jewel felt like cruelly pointing that out to Bunny, but she held her peace.

She even smiled at her mother-in-law politely and her sister Jenny who was sitting beside her. "Oh, how I love weddings, big or small, impromptu or well-planned," Bunny said.

She was speaking to Jenny, but it was loud enough for Jewel to hear.

"I do love weddings, too," Jenny said. "I especially like the details that went into this one. I love saxophone music. I had no idea that Gersham Silver was such a good player."

"I told you he was multi-talented," Bunny said.

"Yes, but to hear it is to believe it," Jenny beamed, "I wonder if I could get him to play at our next Lion's Club fundraiser?"

"I doubt it; he is as shy as anything. Only Jill could have gotten him out of his shell. Speaking of Jill, I was at her place while she was getting ready. She's going to make a beautiful bride," Bunny said. "Just like Shay. I have two perfect daughters-in-law now. God is good."

Jewel kept her head straight ahead.

Jenny reached past Bunny and touched her hand. "Bunny can't count; she has three perfect daughters-in-law. Forgive her."

Jewel didn't react. She was used to Bunny by now. They traded barbs. It was their thing. At first, it had hurt. Now it didn't.

After their first summer, when Mercedes warned her about being a doormat, Jewel gave as good as she got. It had taken some getting used to standing up to Bunny, but she anticipated the snarky comments now.

"I'm happy Bunny has at least two good daughters-in-law; she is doing much better than I am with a zero-good mother-in-law."

Bunny bristled. "What did I tell you about her, Jenny?"

Jenny chuckled. "She gives as good as she gets. She's sassy and pretty and no doormat."

"I never said any of that," Bunny said.

Jewel chuckled. "But I bet you were thinking it."

"Okay, that's enough," Bobby walked in and slid into the pew between them. "I couldn't hear what you two were saying, but I know it wasn't good."

****

Larry and Jill had a vibrant dance floor.

"There was never a dull moment at that party," Jewel said after removing her makeup, taking a shower, and pulling on her boy shorts and tank top.

Rory had showered before she did, and he was lounging in bed, half asleep. "I set the alarm for six. I don't want to be late for work."

Jewel cuddled beside him. "One would think that since you are the owner's son, you would get to show up whenever you want."

Rory chuckled and pulled her closer. "My dad has no reservations about firing me if I start acting entitled. Besides, I want to start working on our place in earnest now that I am here."

"Good," Jewel murmured, "no more mandatory family meals with Bunny; she gets upset when I don't show up like you all do. When I live in my own place, I can make it so I don't have to see her for months. Dealing with your mom is exhausting."

"And that's why I want to complete our house as soon as possible," Rory said. "Can you hang in there for a little bit longer?"

"I will." Jewel kissed him on the cheek. "Now, good night Mr. Nelson. It was a nice party, and I liked dancing with you."

"Good night Mrs. Nelson." Rory kissed her on her forehead. "I dread you going to work and having all those guys lusting after you."

"No need to worry," Jewel said sleepily. "I lust after you alone. You are everything I need. There is no place like you."

Chapter Thirteen

"I can't believe we're working at Kent and Moses," Kenny screamed.

Jewel smothered a yawn; she was still tired from last night's party. "It's a nice place to work. You'll love it here."

"Look at her acting all nonchalant because she's worked here every summer since her first year at university." Kenny grinned.

"Yup," Jewel nodded. "All thanks to Shay. And I got an in when I impressed the owners with my skills."

"I'm looking forward to working with you," Kenny said.

"Too bad we won't be on the same team," Jewel shrugged. "I think they'll be placing me with Marcel Dixon. At least we'll be on the same floor."

They exited the elevator together.

A young lady greeted them at the door. "My name is Francine, and I'm from HR. You are the two newest members of team Kent and Moses. Jewel, of course, is familiar with our operation."

Jewel nodded. "Hey, Francine."

"And you probably won't need the tour," Francine said, "because you were with us for four months last year. Nothing much has changed since then. You are assigned to Marcel Dixon's team."

Just as she thought. Jewel said out loud, "okay."

"Let me walk you to your office, and then I'll give Kenny a tour of this floor, and then we'll come back and check on you."

"Nice," Kenny said. She was brimming over with excitement.

Jewel was a tad bit apprehensive. As Francine said, she knew the place already. She had worked there two summers.

She knew about Marcel Dixon and his past relationship with Shay. He was also known around the office as somewhat of a womanizer. Not that she would have a problem resisting him, she just did not want to be constantly harassed.

Marcel was the only one in the team office when she stepped in.

He was staring at his computer, and he looked up at her. "Hey, Jewel!"

They had never spoken. When he had joined the staff last year, she had been on her way out to do her final year of university. No doubt he had read her file, looked at her pictures, and perused all her social media by now.

"Hello, Marcel!" Jewel said politely.

"The others are not here yet," Marcel said. "We just finished a project. It was one of those bloodsucking projects that had us up late; we could have used someone like you. I see on your file you are the coding queen."

"Someone actually wrote that?" Jewel asked.

"Yup," Marcel nodded, "a glowing review from the

managing director herself. All the team leaders haggled to have you on their team. I got you because there was a vacancy. They couldn't argue with that."

"Oh wow." Jewel grinned. "All I did was casually point out a line of error when passing by an office. I wasn't even working on the project."

"That was a multimillion-dollar app," Marcel said, "our best minds were on it, and it wasn't working. You casually strolled in as a summer worker still in her second year of university and pulled the whole team out of their misery.

"I am almost sorry that our next job is not as complicated as the last one." Marcel frowned, "I want to know what all the hype is about."

Jewel swallowed. "Okay then."

Marcel laughed, "don't look so scared. It's always a team effort."

"Okay, we are finished with this floor," Francine said at the door, "are you settling in okay?"

"She's fine," Marcel grinned, "I may have told her that I wish we were going to work on a hard project for her team initiation."

Kenny gave Jewel a thumbs-up while looking at Marcel with googly eyes. Jewel knew she was going to get an earful about how handsome he was.

And he was handsome. And he knew it.

He showed her to her desk. Six desks were in the room; they were wider than normal, with two banks of monitors.

There were no private offices.

If you wanted to make a private phone call, you had to go to the break room or outside if you didn't want anyone listening in.

You needed to get along with your team members. From what Jewel could remember, it was possible to spend hours and hours together trying to wrangle computer code.

"Since I read your file, I have been wondering," Marcel said when she sat down in her chair and spun it around. "Why did you get married so early?"

"Because we love each other and saw no point in waiting," Jewel said.

"Hmm." Marcel looked skeptical. "What do you ladies find so attractive about these Nelson men?"

Jewel didn't respond. What was she to say?

"I know your mom, you know," Marcel said. "I visit Sensuous City a time or two."

Jewel nodded. "That's nice. But I don't work at Sensuous City. I work here. What's on the team agenda?"

"Straight to business," Marcel laughed. "I like that. I think we'll get on well."

****

The week got steadily busier for both her and Rory. It was like one minute they were in school, and the next minute they were at work. But work was infinitely more challenging than school.

The light project that Marcel had so eloquently bragged about had turned into a bigger project. And their team was being pressured to pass it along the pipeline quickly. Jewel knew what it was like working at Kent and Moses for the summer, but they had separate programs for their summer workers.

This was the big leagues. And while it was exhilarating and thrilling, it turned out to be exhausting. Added to that, she hardly saw Rory.

His first days at work were also busy. Saturday and Sunday couldn't come soon enough for Jewel.

She drove to Sensuous City on Friday night and was plunged into an epic showdown. She walked into Pearl's office intending to complain about how hectic her life had suddenly become when she found Pearl and Leonard in the middle of a quarrel.

"Now, why would you want to leave?" Leonard asked just as she got to the office entrance. "You have it good here, Pearl."

Jewel cleared her throat. "Is this a bad time?"

"Did you know your mother wanted to leave this place?" Leonard asked her aggressively. Jewel shook her head and looked at Pearl with shock in her eyes. She knew Pearl had plans two years ago and those plans had fallen through the cracks, she didn't know that she was still actively working on getting out.

"Ah, you didn't even tell your daughter?" Leonard said. "I was right. This is not a well-thought-out plan, Pearl. What does 'going out' on your own mean? There is no going out on your own. There is no leaving me!"

"Leonard, I'm going to say this again," Pearl said. "I am not a slave. I am a woman with autonomy. I should have the right to leave anytime I want to."

"You know, it would have been better for you," Leonard said threateningly, "if you had just packed your bags and disappeared."

Both Pearl and Jewel stilled. He wasn't even trying to hide the threat.

"But notice, Pearl, if you leave here, you can't stay in the house I built for you on my father's land."

Pearl swallowed.

"That car you drive, is mine. And that education that your kid has? She has to pay for it now."

"You said two years," Pearl protested. "You said she could

pay you back in two years."

"I haven't even gotten my first paycheck yet," Jewel said. "This is my first week."

"You know what?" Leonard grimaced. "I'm a generous man. You have six months. If you don't pay me back in six months, Jewel, you move in with me. You're a pretty girl. You'll be my prettiest yet."

Jewel froze. "I'm married. And how will I get millions of dollars in six months?"

"Don't know, don't care. Blame your mother," Leonard said. "I don't like changes. Now I'm going to have to find someone to run Sensuous City. That's a shame since nobody did it better than Pearl."

"Why are you so selfish?" he asked Pearl.

Pearl folded her arms under her bosom and didn't say a word. "I only told you I was leaving because I wanted you to replace me with someone else. I thought it was only fair to give you notice."

"I don't know what you're doing, Pearl, but this isn't what I expected of you. As for you, Miss," he looked at Jewel, "you'll be my girlfriend by the end of November. Maybe you can also run Sensuous City!"

Jewel swallowed. "Why am I being dragged into this?"

"It's all your mother's fault," Leonard said. "If Pearl stayed, I wouldn't require you to pay me back at all. But since she is leaving, it should take you just two years to work it off in my bed. Your mother knows it wasn't a bad place to be."

He walked out of the office and then turned around. "If you're leaving, Pearl, I want you gone by tomorrow. Anything that is mine, you return, okay?"

****

It's a good thing I took out a loan for your car," Pearl said. "Or else you wouldn't be able to drive me home. Now that I am out of a job, I am afraid that you will have to make the payments."

Jewel nodded. "Sure thing."

She was still shell-shocked, it was almost eight o'clock on a Friday night, and they were heading to Cascade Hills.

"I'm happy that you're leaving, but what are you going to do?" she asked.

"I'll call Chex Hastings and ask for a job. I'll tell him I quit my job for real this time. I'll stay with Madge. She lives in a mansion in a gated community. Leonard can't get to me there. He doesn't have the clout."

"How long have you been planning this?" Jewel asked.

"I've been plotting to leave for years," Pearl said. "The first job I had lined up a couple years ago didn't work out. I have had it up to here with this job. I want a change of pace. I just couldn't take it one more day, especially after hearing Leonard nitpick about one thing or another. When you're about to scratch someone's eyes out, it's time to leave your job. Violence is not the answer."

Jewel chuckled. "I'll keep that in mind."

"Yup, when your job becomes a bloodsucking, soul-wrecking wasteland, get out and save yourself and your sanity. You should have seen his face when I said I was leaving," Pearl said with satisfaction. "I will always cherish that look."

"Where am I going to get four million dollars by November?" Jewel asked. "Leonard is crazy if he thinks I'll become his mistress."

"He doesn't mean it, it's just a bully tactic to get me to stay," Pearl said. "He knows I would fight tooth and nail to keep you safe. But I am not going to be cowed into staying this time. You are married, and you have a good job. You will pay him back somehow."

"I don't want Rory to know about this," Jewel said fretfully, "I couldn't ask him to pay my school fees."

"You'll figure something out." Pearl patted her on the knee. "You have Lester and Rory's people or a bank loan… if push comes to shove, swallow your pride and ask for the money."

"Or that app that I created with Kenny in my final year," Jewel said. "I could find a buyer. It's a viable app."

"You see," Pearl said, "you have it covered. I am not worried about you; that is why this is the right time to go."

Chapter Fourteen

Something was going on with Jewel. Rory couldn't quite put his finger on it. He didn't know what had her so troubled, but he was alarmed about it, and she denied that anything was wrong.

He wasn't used to her lying to him like that. She said it wasn't work. It wasn't home either. Bunny had made one of her stinging remarks to Jewel, and she had just accepted it without a retort. It had shocked them all.

Rory walked into his mother's office. She had requested a meeting with him. So far, two official weeks at Nelson Construction had shown him that his family needed his expertise. Last year, he had threatened his mother to leave, to not be a part of Nelson Construction when he left university.

He had told her he would start his own thing unless she showed Jewel a better attitude. She had tried. He didn't think it was going to get any better.

These days she kept her barbs to a minimum, and she

wasn't outrightly hostile like she was that first summer they had returned home. She was on a phone call while he waited on her, and Rory took the liberty of remembering.

After the speech at dinner, where Bunny had begrudgingly welcomed Jewel, they had done a pretty good job of avoiding each other. Bunny had been especially gratified that Jewel had a job.

"At least she's not work-shy or a gold digger." Bunny had said at the time, "not that we have seen any signs of that yet. Do you know how she's paying next year's school fees?"

Rory had no idea and had asked Jewel.

"My uncle will take care of it," Jewel had said. And that was that.

He knew her uncle took care of her school fees, and her aunt took care of her living arrangements and pocket money. Even when they had moved off campus and rented an apartment, her aunt had sent her portion of the rent.

So far, Jewel had not impacted his finances one bit. And it was something that they never discussed.

Bunny hung up the phone and looked at him and smiled.

"How is it going?"

"It's going great," Rory said. "I think you guys reserved quite a few projects for me so that when I started here, you could give me a lot of work."

"I wish that were so," Bunny said. "But the truth is that we really needed an on-staff architect. Someone who is dedicated to our company. Larry's more into the interior, and Jeremiah is not a specialist."

Rory nodded. "I understand that. That's why I did it in college, so that I could come here and help out."

Bunny nodded. "About that, your graduation is in October, and we were thinking of throwing a party for you and Jewel. Though I don't like it, she is family."

Rory smiled. I knew you'd come around.

"Don't celebrate so fast," Bunny said. "I called Sensuous City to speak to Pearl, thinking she might have had something in mind regarding the party, only to find out that Pearl is no longer there."

"She isn't?" Rory raised an eyebrow. "Why hadn't Jewel told him this?"

"I spoke instead to a lady named Trixie, who sounded overwhelmed and mad at Pearl for leaving her to handle everything. Anyway, Trixie has no filter and gave me a long rundown of her boss, Leonard, and Pearl and their unique dynamics. Being the nosy person I am, I decided to investigate them."

"Whoa, hold on a second," Rory said. "Investigate? Again, Mom, why?"

"Yes, investigate," Bunny said. "And you're not going to like this. Leonard Crooks is not a man you want to be near in any way. He paid for Jewel's education. Nothing for that man is free. The question is, why did he do it, and what does he want in return for his investment in her? And how will this affect you?"

"I knew that girl was bad news," Bunny said. The women who leave his employ don't stay alive for long.

"What?" Rory asked.

"When they leave him, they die mysteriously; one died by drowning, it was ruled as suicide, and the other died when she lost control of her car and crashed into a wall. Not to mention that that man has a way of weeding himself into these women's lives, becoming indispensable to them, and then ruling them with an iron fist.

"And by indispensable, I mean he pays for their private education; he buys them cars, houses. It's like a contract they can't leave."

"This can't be right," Rory whispered. "Jewel has never said anything about this. We have never talked about it."

"That's what happens when you get married without any plans or thought; you don't know your spouse the way you should," Bunny said. "We always thought that Jewel was financially independent and could stand on her own. That's one of the reasons I never said anything after last year. I was like, 'Why am I stressing over this girl? She's not a gold digger; she loves my son.'"

"I thought I was beginning to like her, but this makes me question everything. Did she target you? Is this all a long game she's playing? Does she know about your trust fund? Does she know that as soon as you turn twenty-one, you'll have access to a lot of money?"

"How would she know that?" Rory asked. "Nobody outside of our family knows this."

"I bet she thought she won the lottery when she married you," Bunny said feverishly. "After all, you're Bobby Nelson's son."

"I don't think she thought about that," Rory said. "And I'm the one who proposed."

"Oh, yes, you're the one who drove the dagger into my heart," Bunny said. "Don't remind me."

"I didn't bring it up; you did," Rory pointed out patiently. "It's something you frequently do."

"Nevertheless, I find this threatening to our family," Bunny cleared her throat. "And because of that, I'll be watching your girl."

"What do you mean you'll be watching her?" Rory asked.

"I mean, I'll be watching her," Bunny said.

"We could just ask her what's the situation," Rory said. "It's not that complicated, Mom. Did her uncle pay for her school fees? If yes, then what should she do in return? That's all."

Bunny shrugged, "Okay, you do things your way, I'll do things mine. About that party, you can ask Jewel who she wants to invite, apart from her Webb family. I might not approve of her, but I'm happy that you have achieved this milestone."

"Thanks, Mom." Rory got up.

****

Rory texted Jewel as soon as he left the office. "Lunch at one, Nelson Construction Cafeteria or Bricknell Bar?"

Bricknell Bar was a high-end place that Jewel adored.

She replied, "Bricknell Bar, of course."

Rory vowed to make lunch a thing for them. He was more flexible with his time. There was no reason they couldn't do lunch regularly. Things were settling in for both of them.

Jewel walked into the bar in her black pants, white top, and high ponytail swinging behind her as she walked.

More than one guy turned around to stare. Not for the first time, Rory felt lucky. She had said yes to him.

Would she have said yes if he wasn't Rory Nelson?

It was his mother's doubts creeping into his mind. He had no reason to doubt Jewel. She reached down and kissed him when she came to the table.

"I may not be the most perceptive person, but I know something is wrong. What's up? You know you can talk to me about anything."

Jewel rotated her neck and then rubbed it. "My mom left Sensuous City, which has put us in somewhat of a crisis."

"What crisis?" Rory asked. "Your crisis is my crisis." He laced his fingers with hers.

Jewel sighed heavily. "Well, my uncle took back everything

from her. She packed her bags, went to Kingston, and is laying low."

"Why would she need to lay low?" Rory asked.

Jewel looked around and whispered, "Well, Leonard is not the most forgiving person. He doesn't like change, and they had an unspoken deal."

"An unspoken deal?" Rory asked.

"Yup, the deal is that she lived in the house he built and ran his business, and in return, she would stay forever."

"That's unreasonable," Rory said.

"And that is Leonard," Jewel said.

"So what was your deal with him?" Rory asked.

"That I pay him back for my schooling after two years," Jewel said.

"Oh," Rory looked at her. "How much is it? We should pay him back now."

"I have it sorted," Jewel said. "I just need to work on this app that Kenny and I were doing, and I can easily pay him back by his deadline."

"Don't hesitate to come to me for anything. Okay?" Rory said. "Your problems are my problems. Remember that. We're in this together."

"Okay," Jewel nodded. "I'm starving. Let's eat."

Something was still not quite right. Rory inhaled shakily. He would wait her out, she would eventually tell him.

Chapter Fifteen

Jewel walked into the office a little later than usual. She had overslept. Only waking up when she felt Rory kiss her goodbye. He had an extra early start, and she hadn't slept through the night. She had tossed and turned, the looming threat of Leonard's ultimatum hanging over her head.

That and she hadn't confided the true state of affairs with Rory. That her two-year deadline had shrunken to six months.

She didn't want him to pay her bill. In her mind, it would be unfair to him. The app she built with Kenny in their final year was her only hope. She didn't know who to ask about it. Surely it would be a conflict of interest to ask anyone at Kent and Moses about selling an app.

She had been feverishly praying for a breakthrough. She was due a miracle, and she was going to claim it; she had faith bigger than a mustard seed. Pastor Brewster told her you don't need anyone to dictate your relationship with

God. Believe in him, believe that he can do all things, and big things will happen for you.

Big things can happen for me, Jewel whispered to herself. Big things, huge things, grand things.

Marcel was on the phone when she walked into the office. Susan, Kia, Paul, Guthrie, and Noah, the whole team, were already at their desks, steaming cups of coffee in front of them, already hard at work. They must have gotten a new assignment.

Marcel looked up when she walked in. And waved at her, probably acknowledging her tardiness.

Despite the rumors, Marcel did act professionally around her. After the first day, when she had made it clear that she didn't care to talk about Sensuous City or that her mother worked there, he hadn't mentioned anything personal again.

He was talking loud enough on the phone for all of them to hear. So it wasn't a personal call. Maybe it was in-house with another team leader.

Jewel tuned out his conversation and searched her bag for her headphones when the conversation turned interesting.

"I'm sorry, Richard," Marcel said. "But I think your app would be too small a project for Kent and Moses. You can always buy a generic project management app."

When he hung up, he smiled at her. "Hey, Miss Queen of Coding, we have an absolute doozy of a project. Check your queue and dig in."

Jewel nodded. "Sorry I am late."

"You can make it up to us by pushing the team along with your brilliance."

Jewel nodded and turned on her computer.

Then she looked across at Marcel. "What sort of project management app does your friend need?"

"Ah, you heard the conversation," Marcel grinned,

"Richard owns a construction firm, much like your father-in-law's setup. He desperately needs a project management app."

"We did a project management app for our final project at Uni," Jewel said. "Kenny and I worked on it as a team."

"How far along is it?" Marcel asked.

"It's functional," Jewel said. "We would have to customize it for a specific company, though. We'll need some information to get it done for that business."

"Okay, sounds good," Marcel smiled. "I will set up a meeting when he returns from the UK."

Jewel squeaked. "Really?"

"Yes, really, I've seen your work. I expect it to be immaculate," Marcel winked at her. "But this arrangement is not free. I will need my commission for setting up the buyer with the seller."

"That's no problem," Jewel said. "It depends on what your commission is anyway."

"Just five percent," Marcel said.

"That sounds reasonable," Jewel nodded.

"I like the way you think," Marcel said. "You are shaping up to be a great businesswoman. Is Kenny as intelligent and quick as you?"

"Of course," Jewel knit her brow.

"Is she single?" Marcel asked.

"She is," Jewel said.

"Good," Marcel smiled.

"Bad," Susan interjected. "Don't let him near your friend. He's bad news. He's a love rat."

"Kenny can handle herself," Jewel said. "She eats men like Marcel for breakfast."

"Intriguing," Marcel smiled. "I like her already."

Jewel chuckled.

She was feeling suddenly lighthearted with relief. She would have a way to pay off her uncle after all.

****

Jewel had sent Kenny an SOS; Kenny had arrived in the nearly empty cafeteria, looking slightly frazzled.

"I'll have what you're having," she pointed to Jewel's mocha.

"I anticipated that, and I got one for you right here," she pushed the cup over to Kenny. "How is it going?"

"My team was short-circuiting," Kenny snorted. "We came upon a glitch and couldn't work it out. They sent the code to Shay, who is on maternity leave, and an hour later, she sent it back—fixed and improved."

Jewel chuckled.

"You know Shay, personally?" Kenny said in reverent tones. "Is she totally human?"

"Totally," Jewel nodded, "and awesome. When she comes back, you'll get to know her, and you'll love her."

"Looking forward to that," Kenny said. "I'm also looking forward to moving out of the house—my sisters are driving me crazy. Unfortunately, I have many things to do with the next six months' paychecks."

"Now we're talking," Jewel said excitedly. "That's why I sent you the SOS. I heard about a way for us to make some bank off our final project."

"I actually thought you heard about Audra's pregnancy, and you were going to badger me about who the father is like everyone else is doing," Kenny said.

"Say what now?" Jewel asked, shocked. "Audra, with her perfect plan, is pregnant? I wondered how I hadn't seen her much in the last year. I figured her med degree was kicking her butt."

"I don't know why I brought it up," Kenny said. "Let's talk about making some money."

"I can't believe this," Jewel ignored Kenny. "Audra, who has everything planned and organized down to a T? Audra, who was going to finish med school earlier than anyone else in her family and marry a doctor and be a power couple like her mom and dad, that Audra?"

Kenny nodded. "That Audra."

"Goodness, if ever there was news guaranteed to make me forget about making money and rescuing me from my crap situation with Leonard, this is it. Is she even going to graduate?"

"No," Kenny said. "She flunked the last year. She doesn't know if she wants to do medicine anymore, and she's not saying who is the father of her baby."

Jewel nodded. "For Audra to give up her dreams and plans for some man, he must be amazing."

"Or, he could be totally a shocker," Kenny chuckled. "Maybe that's why she's not showing him off. I have a theory that maybe it's one of the guys she met at one of her leadership club meetings and fell head over heels in love with. You know she insisted on rubbing shoulders with the right people, and that club was full of the pretentious."

"I should visit her," Jewel said.

"She's not here in Trelawny," Kenny shrugged. "Her parents shipped her off to the US to have her kid there and sort out her life."

"I see," Jewel nodded. "Knowing Audra, she'll land on her feet."

"She will," Kenny said. "I'm never worried about Audra. So, tell me about us."

Jewel leaned forward. "Well, I overheard Marcel talking

about a project management app for a construction company. He was telling the client that it was too small a job for this company. I said, 'That's what Kenny and I did for our final project.' Marcel said, 'Oh really, great. I'll set up a meeting, and we can talk business.'"

"Eek!" Kenny squealed.

"I know," Jewel grinned. "I have been smiling at weird times since we sorted that out. The question is, have you finished working on that feature we talked about last week?"

"Yes, I did," Kenny nodded. "How about you? Did you design the landing page to look sleeker like we discussed?"

"Never got round to it," Jewel said. "I wasn't expecting this, but I'll get on it as soon as I reach home tonight."

"I'm excited," Kenny grinned. "We put a lot of hard work into this app. Didn't I tell you it would pay off one day, didn't I?"

"Yes, you did," Jewel said. "And I am happy they made us do market research for the project to show that there was a real need for the app. Even though I complained at the time."

"With the way we've designed it and how user-friendly it is, we can either sell it to the mass market or offer it to one interested buyer for lots of money."

"It's mind-boggling," Jewel said excitedly. "We need to do some final testing, and then we can decide."

Kenny looked at her watch. "I have to run; keep me posted."

Jewel nodded and was about to get up too when her phone rang. It was Bunny.

Bunny rarely called her phone; whenever she did call, it was chiefly because Rory wasn't answering his phone.

She inhaled before answering.

There was no preamble with Bunny; she didn't waste time

on greetings.

"Jewel, I wanted to let you know that I'm planning a graduation party for Rory next month. I'll be sending out the invitations soon. Since you are graduating, too, I guess it will be a dual party. I did mention it to him several weeks ago; you have not sent in your list of invitees."

Jewel grimaced. Rory had told her, and she had ignored it. It was such a begrudging inclusion; it was insulting, really.

She wanted to rebut by saying, So sorry, dear Bunny, but my cousin Lester already suggested a party at my grandmother's house to celebrate my graduation where all sides of my family can congregate and have fun, with nobody excluded.

Instead, she cleared her voice of any petulance and tried to sound friendly. It's something she was trying out these days with Bunny.

"That sounds great, Bunny. Thank you for thinking of including me."

"I'll be inviting all of Rory's friends and family, of course, but I don't think it would be appropriate for the Webb part of your family to attend. Please submit your invite list, excluding them, to my secretary by Friday."

And then something in Jewel snapped, and the rival party fantasy reared its head, and she couldn't help sticking it to Bunny.

"Well," she cleared her throat, "my family, mainly my cousin Lester, are already planning a party for me."

Jewel didn't know how the lie didn't choke her. "I will invite my friends and family to that one. Lester and Kristine have no restrictions on who I can invite to a party in my honor."

"When is this party?" Bunny asked stonily.

"After graduation, at his house in the hills," Jewel said.

"It's a lovely house with an almost 360-degree view of the mountains. It once belonged to his sister Octavia."

Bunny hung up the phone with not even a goodbye.

Jewel chortled with glee. She could imagine Bunny's face right now, and then she sobered up. She needed to call Lester and beg him to host a graduation party for her to save face.

She dialed his number hurriedly and started talking quickly before she could lose her confidence.

"So I got upset at Bunny because she said I can't invite any of the Webb side of my family to her graduation party that she is throwing for Rory and by default me, of course, because I guess it would look bad. I told her you would be throwing one for me at your mansion in the hills, where I can invite all my family and friends."

Lester hooted with laughter. "When is the exact date of the graduation again?"

"October 10 at 10 am," Jewel said, crossing her fingers.

"Okay," Lester said, "I will hire a caterer and an event planner. I will make arrangements for all the family members who can travel to Kingston for the party. We'll attend the ceremony virtually at the house because I know invitations are limited. Then when you arrive with your friends, we'll have a party that will make Bunny's look like a wake in comparison."

Jewel sighed in relief. "Thank you so much, Lester."

"No problem," Lester said. "This is an excuse for my mother and aunt Edna to come and see the new place. It will be a mini family reunion, and I am really proud of you for finishing university."

Chapter Sixteen

"**I** dislike that girl with a passion," Bunny said. She walked from one end of the kitchen to the other while Bobby and Mercedes watched her.

"I don't understand it." Mercedes said, "I guess the age-old question, 'Can people hate other people for no reason,' is finally answered. Yes, they can. And passionately too."

"I didn't say I hated her, but I dislike her strongly, and today only confirmed it," Bunny said in despair. "She is throwing a rival party for her graduation, and she is using Lester to do it just because she knows it will hurt me."

Bobby nursed a cup of tea in his hands and leaned back in his chair. "Here we go again. Bunny has been talking about this rival party all week. I, for one, am sick of it, and I am going to bed."

He stood up. "Talk some sense into her, Mercedes. I may not be a counselor or psychologist, but even I can see that this is not normal behavior."

Mercedes watched her mother as she paced the floor. "Ma, what's the real reason you're so mad?"

"That's the real reason," Bunny said. "Jewel is throwing a rival party with her family, which includes the Webbs. She loves pitting Lester against me. Did you hear her the other night pointing out how Cerise looks like me, but Anjou looks like Lester? She says stuff like that to hurt me."

Mercedes cupped her chin. "It is true, though. Anjou looks like his biological grandfather, and Jewel, to be honest. He looks more like her child than Shay's. How are you planning to treat him?"

"What are you talking about, Mercedes?" Bunny glared at her daughter. "I won't treat Anjou any differently than I treat Cerise. I love him to shreds."

"Good," Mercedes said. "It's just that it seems a little unfair that you strongly dislike Jewel for being related to Lester Webb when Jeremiah, your son, is related to him too, and now even your grandchildren are shouting that they are Webbs."

"Jewel rubs me the wrong way," Bunny said with a grunt.

"But why?" Mercedes asked. "We have already established that it is not her association with Lester that has you out of sorts with her, so what is it?"

"She looks like Octavia and acts like her, too," Bunny sighed. "It's in the way she walks or sweeps back her hair or even the way she talks."

"Oh?" Mercedes raised her eyebrows. "Who is Octavia?"

"Octavia is the woman that...I don't want to talk about it, especially not with you," Bunny said. "I have kept things in all these years; this reincarnation of Octavia is making me a little crazy, is all. I will be fine."

"You won't be," Mercedes said. "It has been more than two years since Jewel joined the family. Rory loves that woman to pieces. They are not breaking up. You will have to deal with Jewel or lose your son!"

"Not if I can help it," Bunny gritted out. "I still have some aces up my sleeve."

"Mom," Mercedes said softly, "don't tell me you are actively trying to break up Rory's marriage."

"I won't tell you," Bunny said flippantly.

"Then, since you cannot talk to me," Mercedes said, "you should be talking to someone. I have several colleagues that I can recommend, and I suggest that you speak to one soon before you do something that you will regret, something that will tear this family apart."

****

"So this is it," Rory said, standing up in the middle of the batter boards used to outline the house.

"This is it," Jewel said, standing beside him. "Is the house going to be this big?"

"No," Rory chuckled. "They are usually generous with the laying out of the boards. May I give you a tour, Mrs. Nelson?"

"Yes, Mr. Nelson," Jewel chuckled.

"So right this way," Rory said, pointing to a patch of dirt, "is the living room. It's going to be a great space for entertaining guests and relaxing with the family."

"It's so open and bright. I love it!" Jewel said, playing along.

"Rory chuckled and over here is the kitchen. We went with a modern design, but I want us to add traditional elements to make it feel homier."

"It's perfect. I can't wait to cook in here!"

"Through here is the master bedroom. We have a walk-in

closet and a master bath."

"It's beautiful. I love the natural light that comes through the windows. We have a lot of windows, don't we?"

"Of course," Rory said. "The bedroom will overlook the infinity pool as you requested."

"Good," Jewel smiled.

"I aim to please Mrs. Nelson. You are the client. We also have three other bedrooms and a guest bath. Plus, as requested, I added a small office space for you on this side of the house."

Jewel smiled and spun around. "It's more than I ever imagined. I can't wait to move in."

"Me too," Rory said. "I can't wait to see the finished product and make it our home. We should go out tonight and celebrate. Let's do something expensive and dress up too!"

"Okay," Jewel clapped her hands in glee. "Life is looking up."

"Happy to see that you are happy," Rory pulled her closer to him and kissed her.

****

Jewel and Rory walked into the posh Cloud Nine lobby area with their hands intertwined. They were both dressed in formal attire, Jewel was in a little black dress accentuating her curves and Rory in a sharp suit. The place had a resort-like feel and housed three different restaurants.

There was a lobby area to the right and a lounge area with a bar to the left. It had been easy for Rory to get a short notice booking at the main restaurant, which overlooked the bay area. Bunny was friends with the owner, and he would happily accommodate the Nelson family any time they wanted.

They entered the lounge; plush chairs were arranged in circles, and cocktail music played in the background.

"It just feels luxurious in here," Jewel inhaled. "I've always wanted to eat here ever since coming to Bunny's birthday party last year."

"Well, I am happy that we could make it," Rory gripped her hand tighter.

"I can't believe he's here," Jewel groaned. "Of all the nights."

"Who?" Rory looked around.

"Uncle Leonard," Jewel sighed.

"Where is he?" Rory asked.

"The big guy with the group of people around him. He always has to be the center of attention."

"We should say hi," Rory murmured. "I have never met him. He is your uncle, your family."

"Step uncle," Jewel corrected. "And I didn't grow up interacting with him much. My mother made sure of that. We have a hi and bye kind of relationship."

"Well, let's go then," Rory whispered.

But it was too late, Leonard had spotted them.

"Jewel! Come here and give your uncle a hug!" he shouted.

"He's half drunk," Jewel muttered. "He sounds way too mellow for my liking. Do not let go of my hand."

Rory nodded. They walked over to Leonard, Jewel with a forced smile on her face. He pulled her in for a hug, dragging Jewel away from Rory, and held on for a little too long. She tried to pull away, but Leonard's grip was strong.

Rory could see the discomfort on Jewel's face and stepped in. "Excuse me, sir," he said firmly. "I think it's time for you to let go of my wife."

Leonard finally released Jewel and stumbled back. "Oh, excuse me," he slurred. "I didn't realize, so you are the husband? Good God, he's just a boy!"

"Bobby Nelson's son!" one of the men in the group said with a warning.

"Oh," Leonard nodded, "good family."

He backed away from Jewel and Rory. "Well, nice to meet you..."

"Rory," Rory supplied helpfully.

"Jewel, you never said you were married into the Nelson family. Look at that," Leonard muttered. "Have you talked to your mother?"

"Not lately," Jewel said truthfully. Pearl had been texting her instead from a burner phone. It was all cloaks and daggers, like they were in an intriguing movic. It would have been funny if it wasn't so serious.

"Well then, nice to meet you, Rory. And nice to see you, Jewel."

They quickly made their way to the restaurant.

"I don't like him," Rory said.

"Join the club," Jewel muttered.

"Is he dangerous?" Rory asked.

"I think so," Jewel said. "He's okay when things are going his way, but when they don't, he is probably murderous."

"Goodness. Are you safe?" Rory asked, concerned.

"Yes," Jewel shook her head. "I think so. He wants my mother to come back to him. She left him and his business. I don't think he cares about me much as a person. He just wants Pearl back. I don't think she is safe, though, because he doesn't let things go. My mom knows who she is dealing with and has taken precautions."

"Well, let's forget about him then," Rory said. "It's our date night. We're at a fancy restaurant. We have Audra's pregnancy to speculate about and our rival graduation parties."

Jewel laughed. "So, you heard about Audra."

"Everybody has heard about Audra," Rory said. "I asked Camden if the baby was his, and he laughed so hard he choked."

"I wonder who it could be though?" Jewel said.

"None of our business," Rory chuckled. "I'm going to tell my mom about it. She'll have a fit. She's always wanted me to marry Audra."

"Oh my," Jewel grinned. "Bunny has too many things on her plate right now. Her ideal girl for you is pregnant for an unknown man, and your wife is throwing a rival graduation party at her ex's house. I love it, let's drink to that."

Chapter Seventeen

October started with a bang, and the rival parties was the topic of many heated discussions around the dinner table. Jewel had ensured that she wasn't a part of any of those dinners. In fact, she was taking great pains to avoid Bunny. It wasn't hard to do, she was swamped with work, and she still had to tweak the app.

Rory insisted on joining his family for communal meals, and he reported to her faithfully on the state of things.

"So the plan is that Larry and Jill will be coming to your party; they accepted the invite," Jewel chuckled. "Good old Larry, he's not even the tiniest bit phased by his mom and her threats of loyalty. I'm surprised that Jill defied Bunny and accepted though. I know Bunny has been putting it out there that going to my party is high treason."

Rory chuckled. "Jill is nice up to a point. She thinks it's balanced if she goes to your party and then comes to mine. She reassured Bunny that the cakes at my party would be far better than yours because she will be doing them."

Jewel laughed. "I don't doubt that for a minute."

"Jeremiah and Shay are going to your party as well," Rory went into the wardrobe for socks. It was oddly much cooler than a typical September. He settled in the bed beside Jewel and looked over at her.

"I can't believe Jeremiah is coming. How is Bunny handling that?" Jewel asked, intrigued.

"She's not," Rory grimaced. "When he said he and Shay were going, mom got up and walked out of the dining room. I haven't seen her since."

"What did your father do?" Jewel asked.

"Dad said he would come to your party, too," Rory replied, "but I should tell you that he's declining the invite with much reluctance. He has to stay away to keep mom from going insane."

Jewel laughed. "You have the best dad. I wouldn't expect him to come. I sent them the invites just to make Bunny's hackles rise."

"I know," Rory said sleepily. "Love you."

"Love you too, hun," Jewel reached down and kissed him. "I can't wait for this stupid rival party thing to be over. I don't know why I started it."

"You wanted to one-up my mom for being snarky and dismissive of you and your family," Rory smiled. "It was a good move. Hats off to Lester for going through with it."

"He'll be so happy to know that Jeremiah and Shay will be there, and he'll get to see his grandkids," Jewel said.

"He gave up all rights to claim them as family," Rory murmured.

"People make mistakes," Jewel said. "He will be the first to tell you he wished he had handled the whole scenario with Bunny better."

"But if he had handled it better and she hadn't run into my dad to defend her from Lester, I wouldn't be here," Rory said. "I like that I am here."

"Me too," Jewel put away her laptop and snuggled close to him. "I was speaking to Maud Beecher the other day. I saw her on the road while driving home from work and gave her a lift. She said almost the same thing. She said, you can regret the past, but if you made one decision otherwise, you wouldn't be here."

Rory snickered. "Maud Beecher doesn't have all her ducks in a row, if you know what I mean."

"She's fine," Jewel pinched him. "She's just eccentric."

"She needs to stop time traveling," Rory chuckled. "I swear she has infected all of Crimson Hills with her madness."

"She said things will get worse, and then they'll be wonderfully better for us," Jewel continued. "I asked her what she meant, and she said, 'I'll soon find out.'"

"Well, then let's find out," Rory kissed her and then closed his eyes sleepily.

Jewel watched him until he started breathing heavily. He didn't take long to fall asleep.

Just like that, he was out like a light; Jewel wished she had the power to fall asleep so quickly; her brain had to do a thorough churning before she could power down. This was the time she processed several thoughts, like where was Pearl, she hadn't heard from her mom in a couple days. And would she be able to deliver the money to her uncle in time?

She moved out from under Rory's arms and picked up her computer; there was no reason why she should waste her precious waking hours fretting about her future. She needed to fix some things in the app.

****

"I still can't wrap my head around the fact that you two are still together and happy," Camden said to Rory. "Look at Jewel; she's glowing. Blue is definitely her color."

They were standing away from the crowd at the country club where his mother had invited all the influential people in Montego Bay and Trelawny. Jewel was currently cornered by a popular comedian who was talking and gesturing at her. She was laughing.

Camden watched Jewel and shook his head sadly. "I honestly thought she would have ditched you by second year and come to cry on my shoulders. Then I would comfort her in the best way I know how."

"Stop lusting after my wife," Rory said. "She's not ditching me. We mate for life."

"I can't lust after your wife or your sister. I can't do nothing," Camden chuckled. "By the way, Jewel's party yesterday was lit! Jewel's grandmother Edna owned the dancefloor. I can't believe I'm going to say this, but the two grandmothers were the life of the party. They put us to shame. I loved it."

"Don't let my mother hear you say that," Rory whispered. "There were some issues."

"What issues?" Camden lowered his voice and looked around. There was nothing behind them, only the row of trees that opened up to the bright blue sea in the distance.

"She quite inexplicably hates Jewel. Of course, she had hated the family before, but Jewel is probably a daily reminder. I don't know. It has only gotten worse since we moved back here to live."

"Aunt Bunny loves everyone!" Camden said. "I've seen her be cordial and sweet to some dubious people in all the years I've known her."

"You should be a fly on the wall at dinnertime," Rory

chuckled. "When Jewel joins us for dinner, knives are drawn, and the barbs fly. They're like combatants on a battlefield."

"Invite me to dinner!" Camden rubbed his hands together. "I want to see this."

"You like drama too much," Rory snorted. "Besides, the next time we invite you to dinner, we'll be in our own house."

"You've been talking about your own house since you were ten," Camden chuckled. "I feel like, after a decade, you should be done with it by now."

Rory laughed. "We're making steady progress. We're up to the belt course now."

"I'm pleased for you, my friend," Camden smiled. "You know, through the years, people ask me, 'Why are you doing law, Camden? You don't seem like it would be a good fit. You're so happy-go-lucky and not serious.' And I say, 'I do it because of the example of my friend Rory Nelson.'"

"Me?" Rory chuckled. "What did I do?"

"From when you were a tot," Camden said, "you've always been going on about your family business and how your dad would be proud if you did something in construction. He made sure that he created a business for you to work in and build your wealth. He even made sure each of his children would build their own house. It was important to him.

"In a way, my family is the same, four generations of lawyers in the family, from my great-grandfather to me. I see how proud you are of your family business. I envied that, and then something happened, a light went off, and I thought, I should be proud of mine.

"And now I love the law," Camden continued. "I love the idea of continuity and being a fourth generation Byfield lawyer man."

"Well said, Mr. Lawyerman. I am happy to inspire you

to love your family business as I do mine," Rory grinned. "Out of the three of us, Audra surprised me. I thought she was hell-bent on becoming a doctor, but she just ditched her plans without graduating."

"She didn't surprise me," Camden said. "I knew that her heart wasn't in it. The guy she met and fell in love with was just an excuse to break out of her self-imposed prison."

"Why are you guys way over here, being anti-social?" Bunny asked. "Let's go and socialize."

"We should," Camden nodded. "I see Mercedes is alone. My God, she has gotten prettier!"

Bunny rolled her eyes. "I see Camden still has a crush on Mercedes."

Rory laughed.

"Are you and Jewel all right?" Bunny asked with faux concern.

"Why do you ask?" Rory asked.

"She's been standing and giggling with that comedian for a few minutes now," Bunny said. "It just seemed a little odd."

Rory looked at his mother and sighed. "You are hell-bent on causing trouble between us, aren't you?"

"I wouldn't say hell-bent," Bunny grimaced. "I constantly wait for the other shoe to drop with that girl. There is something there, Rory. I know it. I can feel it. And one day, it will be revealed, and I beg God that I don't slip and say, 'I told you so.' I hope to be supportive and kind to you through it all."

"Bonita Nelson," Larry said behind them. "That is a bag of nonsense. What on earth are you telling Rory?"

"Mind your own business, Larry," Bunny sniffed. "Anyway, Rory, this party was not just for celebrating your graduation. I wanted you to network. I have been talking about your superior talents as an architect."

Larry chuckled. "I overheard Mom telling Aunt Jenny that you point at the computer, and poof, a building appears, accurately measured, and precisely what the client wants."

Rory groaned. "Mom, you weren't telling Aunt Jenny that?"

"Well, it's almost true," Bunny said. "The software is amazing these days. Why are you still lurking, Larry?"

Larry grinned. "To keep you honest."

Bunny sighed. "Anyway, Jenny has a huge project in St. Mary. She wants to build a small resort hotel, and she wants you to be in charge of it, Rory."

Rory swallowed. "Really?"

"Ah, your first big project on your own," Larry clapped him on the shoulders. "Congrats, man. Though it's a pity it's for a family member. They are the hardest to please. Trust me when I tell you, this won't be a walk in the park."

Chapter Eighteen

"I told you, Jewel Webb is bad news," Bunny said, waving a paper in the air.

"What's that?" Bobby grunted, looking over his reading glasses at his excited wife.

"My investigations have found out that her mother, Pearl Day, has been bragging that her daughter is beautiful enough to get herself a rich man and not live a hard life like those exotic dancers she used to manage. She told people she's sending her child to university to bag a rich man, just like her sister, Precious, did."

Bobby laughed. "It's not funny, Bobby," Bunny said heatedly. "Gold digging is in her family on both sides. Lester only married his wife for money, Octavia married her husband for his money, and when she couldn't have a child to cement her place in his life, she got desperate and used my mentally ill sister to have one for her. Her aunt, Precious, did the same, and Pearl freely admits it. Jewel has been steeped in this culture for a long, long time."

Bobby sighed. "Bunny, I am tired of asking you to let this go," he said.

"I am happy you are tired, dear because I am not going to let that girl come and break up my family," Bunny sniffed.

"You can't put that on her," Bobby said wearily. "I'd dare say you are managing just fine on your own. This constant pursuit of getting dirt on Jewel to appease some vendetta you have with her cousins will not only push Rory further away from you but also reveal secrets about Mercedes' birth that you claim she isn't supposed to know."

Bunny sat across from Bobby feeling a little deflated about his attitude towards the revelations from her investigations.

"Aren't you even a little bit concerned that Jewel isn't out to damage our son, maybe even permanently?"

"No," Bobby replied. "They have been married for nearly three years now. Jewel has only tried to mind her own business and love her husband.

"But did she target Rory? Does she have genuine feelings for him, or is she playing a long game, pretending not to care about money, and then bam, she'll pounce? She's bad news.

"Jewel is Rory's choice. If he gets hurt, he gets hurt. Leave their relationship alone. You have become that mother-in-law. You need to book several sessions with the therapist that Mercedes suggested to work out your obsession.

"I can't believe you're saying this to me," Bunny said. "My whole family is on Jewel's side. I can't believe it's come to this.

"Oh, Bunny," Bobby looked at her and shook his head. "I wish I had a mirror to show you how you're acting. When you come to your senses, you'll ask me how I allowed you to act like this. I'll tell you I tried, but you wouldn't listen to reason.

Bunny got up. "I'll find something, a smoking gun. You'll see, and then you'll come to me, asking for my forgiveness." She flounced out of the office, leaving Bobby shaking his head.

****

Jewel was sitting at her desk when Marcel texted her. "My place, at six tonight."

"Excuse me?" Jewel texted back.

"The app," Marcel texted. "My friend Richard is here. Bring your friend Kenny. It's strictly business."

Jewel sent him back a thumb's up emoji.

She had made plans to be at Larry and Jill's house for their first dinner party as a couple. She would have to cancel. This app sale was extremely important.

"I guess you'll have to report to your hubby that you will be otherwise engaged for this evening." Marcel walked over to her desk.

"I don't mind being accountable to my husband," Jewel said. "In fact, I like it."

"Ah, the marriage con," Marcel said. "Married people want you to believe that it is so much blissful love and attention. And then, a little bit down the line, it's hell and torture."

"If you feel that way," Jewel said sweetly, "it's a good thing no one wants to marry you."

Susan hollered with laughter.

"Many women want to marry me," Marcel said.

"Many crazy women," Susan said.

"I'll send you directions to my house," Marcel ignored Susan. "I have a meeting. See you all later."

"You shouldn't meet at his house," Susan said snidely. "I don't care what he's saying to get you there."

"This is business," Jewel said. "And I need this to work."

"Your husband will get jealous, and it will break up your relationship," Susan warned.

"We're not that fragile," Jewel shrugged.

"I've never met someone who started out young in a relationship, and it worked long term," Susan shook her head.

"You need to get out more," Jewel chuckled. "I don't know what the future will hold for Rory and me, but I know that a relationship works if both of you want it to work."

****

"**W**here is Jewel?" Bunny asked Rory.

"She has a work thing," Rory said.

Bunny snorted. "Is that what they're calling it these days?"

"Mom," Rory said wearily, "I am tired of these little innuendos and doubt regarding Jewel. Be nicer to my wife. I love her."

"But does she love you?" Bunny asked smugly. "You could do so much better than Jewel. What is Audra doing these days?"

Rory laughed. "She's pregnant and somewhere in the States."

"Goodness, that's terrible," Bunny muttered. "That still doesn't make Jewel good for you."

"She's the best girl for him," Jeremiah came to sit beside him with Anjou in his arms. Because she is who he chose. Mom, we have been discussing this. You need to give Jewel and Rory a chance. Stop interfering in their relationship."

"I'm not interfering!" Bunny exclaimed. "If Anjou grows

up and chooses someone you know will break his heart, you would move heaven and earth to make him see sense."

"Oh God, I hope not," Jeremiah said. "I hope I would have the good sense to allow my son to make his own decisions. If God interfered with all of our decisions, then that wouldn't be autonomy or freedom to choose."

"He interferes when we ask for help," Bunny said.

"And Rory isn't asking for your help." Jeremiah laughed. "Mom, you are going off the deep end."

Bunny glared at him and got up. "I don't like how this family is ganging up on me.

"We don't like how you're ganging up on Jewel," Jeremiah said.

"Thank you for sticking up for me and Jewel," Rory said to Jeremiah.

"Anytime," Jeremiah said. "But in a way, I understand mom's reasoning."

"You do?" Rory asked. "How?"

"Think about it," Jeremiah said. "She had me when she was married to Bobby. She's convinced herself that Lester would probably kill her. Who knows, the man panicked. I don't know his character like that, and I definitely wouldn't be defending him. Anyway, she has deemed him an awful person and lumped his whole family into that bag. She doesn't consider me to be his family -- not in her head. In her head, I am Bobby Nelson's child. When I was born, Dad was there. She thought she had successfully gotten rid of her past with the Webb family, aka Lester Webb. And then you came, talking about him, dating his cousin."

"But you look like them," Rory said. "Your son looks so much like Lester and Jewel. People were asking at the party if Jewel and I had a baby. Mom is not resentful of her grandchild in the least. Why is she taking out her vitriol on a woman who is not as closely related to Lester, like you?"

"I think I know why," Jeremiah sighed. "When I went to Lester's place, he showed me pictures of Octavia. He pulled out his phone and passed it to Rory. I forgot to send them to you and Jewel."

Rory looked at the phone and scrolled through the seven pictures of a woman who looked eerily like his wife. You could see that they weren't exactly lookalikes, but the resemblance was quite strong.

"Send them to me," Rory said. "I wonder what the story is with Mom and Octavia. I heard her whispering with Dad a couple of years ago that they had her to indirectly thank for having Mercedes."

"What?" Jeremiah asked.

Rory shrugged. "I asked Mom, but I got the brush-off. But it has always stuck with me that Mom's resentment towards Jewel was instant and fierce. She has found every excuse in the book to hate on her, and I think it has something to do with Octavia. Maybe you can find out what it is about."

"What are you guys whispering about?" Mercedes came out onto the patio and pulled a chair closer to them. "I don't like you keeping secrets from me."

"Show her the picture," Rory said.

"What picture?" Mercedes frowned.

"This," Jeremiah handed her his phone.

"Ah, Jewel's mom," Mercedes said, scanning the pictures. "They look so much alike."

"No, that's not Jewel's mom," Rory said. "That is Octavia Webb, Lester's sister, Jeremiah's biological aunt, and Jewel's cousin."

"Oh," Mercedes frowned. "Where is she?"

"Dead," Rory said. "According to Jewel, who heard it from Lester, Octavia died in a car accident."

"She didn't just meet in a car accident," Bunny said behind them. "She deliberately drove herself and her ex-husband into a tree. After she lured him into her car. She died instantly, but he survived for a couple of months afterward. The injuries sustained from the accident eventually caused his death."

"Ah, so you know these people," Mercedes said.

"Yes, I know the blood-sucking vampire, Octavia Webb-Monroe,"

Mercedes raised an eyebrow. "Maud Beecher constantly calls me Mercedes Monroe."

"Maud Beecher," Bunny sighed. "How is she talking to you? I told her to stop calling you that years ago and to stay away from you. She's weird, creepy, and doesn't know when to open her mouth."

"She is my new client," Mercedes said. "I find her fascinating."

"Wait a minute," Rory said. "Is Mercedes' father's surname Munroe? Is this somehow linked to Octavia and, by extension, Jewel?"

Bunny glared at him stonily.

"That would be fascinating," Mercedes said, "but Mom has always said she has no idea who my father is. Claudia couldn't tell her at the time."

"That's right," Bunny said. "Your mother, my baby sister, was dying when we got the call that she was in labor. I always thank God that we showed up when we did. She couldn't tell us who she was pregnant for or the circumstances surrounding the birth. I've always suffered the greatest guilt for that."

"But why?" Mercedes said. "Why carry that guilt around?"

"Claudia had developmental problems," Bunny said. "I don't know exactly what she had. It's not as if we had her diagnosed. My parents had eleven of us. She was the last one. The doctors assumed she didn't get enough oxygen at birth. Whatever caused her issues happened when she was born."

"She had several medical problems, and it became apparent that she was going to have developmental problems. Even as an adult, she acted like a child. By the time she was twenty, she wanted to go out and spread her wings. She called me, crying, that she would kill herself if she didn't leave Cascade Hills. I ignored her pleas for independence. I reminded her that she couldn't function in the big, bad world, and that she was safer at home."

"We always assumed she would live at home forever and that when Mom and Dad passed, one of us would have to take her."

"But I underestimated Claudia. I realize now that I didn't take her seriously at all. In a way, I have myself to blame. I treated her as if she was a simple-minded person with special needs who should be grateful to have a family to take care of her. I never considered for a moment that she was a person in her own right, an adult woman who, though she had a disability, had desires and wants just like any other adult woman at twenty-one."

"I've never heard you say that before," Mercedes said. "But you cannot blame yourself for any of it."

"I do blame myself," Bunny sighed. "I was closest to her in age. I was the only sibling she had living in the area, but I still treated her as a kid, an inconvenience."

"You know who didn't treat her like a child? Octavia Webb-Monroe," Rory said. "That's why you hate Jewel so much."

"That opportunistic witch went to Cascade Hills for a visit, befriended Claudia, and took her to Kingston to live.

None of us knew what Claudia was up to in Kingston for close to a year. Every word from her mouth was, 'Octavia says this,' 'Octavia says that.' Octavia took over and caused my sister to die."

"But how?" Mercedes sat up.

"It's unclear," Bunny said. "Octavia could not have kids; that's why she and her husband were divorcing. I think she took Claudia to Kingston to have children for her. And I strongly suspect that Lester was one of the men who was fooling around with Claudia and that he is Mercedes' father."

Everybody gasped. Rory hadn't realized that Larry and Shay had come on the patio while his mother was talking; he was so engrossed in the story. Jill was behind her with a tray in hand and seemed frozen in place.

"Knock, knock," Bobby said from the front of the house. "Where is everybody?"

"Out here," Jill turned around. "I, er, was just about to serve hors d'oeuvres."

"What's going on?" Bobby came onto the patio and looked at them.

"I just heard that I may be Lester Webb's daughter," Mercedes said. "My head is spinning."

"That's just Bunny's version of the story," Bobby said. "I told her not to put it out there. You could belong to Leo Munro, Octavia's ex-husband, or his brother, Cassius."

"Cassius Monroe is a mega-church pastor," Jeremiah whistled. "He is married with five kids, the epitome of black love. They even wrote a book about it."

"Or you could belong to his cousin, Simon Monroe," Bobby said. "The one that runs the family company, who is also married. That's why Bunny and I decided not to tell you that part of the story. We thought it would be best to save you the trouble of searching out your real dad among that group.

"One of them wanted you or Claudia dead. We suspect that she didn't die from natural causes but was deliberately injected with a substance to elevate her heart rate and send her into cardiac arrest. Frankly, it's only because Bunny insisted on going into the birthing room at the last minute that Mercedes is still alive, I suspect. Whoever they paid to kill Claudia did not have the chance to kill you because Bunny was there.

"And because of our suspicions, we vowed never to bring this up again," he said, looking at Bunny.

"But my dear wife has her theories and her biases. Unfortunately, Jewel's resemblance to Octavia has them all riding to the surface.

"Good God," Rory murmured.

"Wow," Mercedes said faintly. "I didn't know my birth or my mother's past was so dramatic."

"There is never a dull moment in this family, is there?" Jill asked faintly. "Where on earth is Jewel?"

"Work," Rory said, still trying to digest everything his mother and father had just said. It had been a lot, and he didn't know how much of it he would tell her. He now understood his mother's animosity toward her and Lester, even after all these years.

"So if Lester is your biological father," Jeremiah said, "that means we are..."

"Biological siblings," Mercedes shrugged. "But none of this matters now, does it? I am twenty-five years old. Life marches on."

Rory looked at her doubtfully. It had to matter to her, and he was sure that when she processed all of this, there would be no marching on for her.

Chapter Nineteen

"I feel like that black SUV is following us," Jewel said. "I've been seeing it a lot lately, wherever I go."

"Which SUV?" Kenny looked behind. "I don't see a SUV. You can't afford to be paranoid now, Jew. We have a lot riding on this. We need your head in the game."

"My head is so in the game, you don't have any idea," Jewel said. "What do we know about Richard Tinsdale?"

"He's young, just thirty-two," Kenny said. "He's a developer with several projects all over the island. He's more into smaller developments than your in-laws are. Low-end developments. And he has a lot of them going on."

"So his company is perfect for our app," Jewel nodded.

"That's right," Kenny said. "And I don't want to get my hopes up."

Jewel drove up to Marcel's house. It was a nice place, with a palm tree-lined driveway and a profusion of red and white bougainvillea at the front.

"Richard Tinsdale is a handsome guy, from what I have seen of his pictures," Jewel said. "Just remember your speech about having your head in the game."

"Ah yes, I have seen the pictures," Kenny said. "And yes, I have asked around if he is single and straight, but no one seems to know. His private life is private. So I may drool, but I can keep my cool."

They had a chuckle together before they alighted from the car. Marcel came out and greeted them at the door.

"Hello, ladies. You can step this way. I thought we'd meet in the dining room," Marcel said.

Jewel and Kenny stepped inside. Richard was already seated and got up to shake their hands eagerly. He had an open computer in front of him.

"When you said, 'Jewel and Kenny,' I was expecting a guy and girl team," he said, looking at both of them.

Kenny grinned. "I get that all the time. My father's name was Kenneth, and my parents thought it would be fun to name all four of us girls starting with 'Ken.' I am Kenny, and my sisters are Kendrea, Kenisha, and Kennice. I got plain old 'Kenny,' I guess they got creative after I was born since I was the first one."

"Interesting," Richard said, looking at her appreciatively.

Marcel cleared his throat. "So, can we talk shop?"

"Sure," Jewel smiled. "I tweaked the app to fit in with what you asked, Richard, and I think you'll love this." She opened her laptop.

Richard rubbed his hands together. "I can't wait! Let's do this."

****

Jewel arrived home well past 10 o'clock. Rory was already

in bed, probably agonizing over his first solo project for his aunt Jenny.

She was over the moon happy. Richard Tinsdale liked the app so much that he was willing to pay millions for the rights to use it.

It hadn't quite sunk in yet.

Jewel and Kenny had acted polite throughout the meeting, but when they were in the parking lot, they looked at each other and screamed with joy.

She was bursting to tell Rory, but she wouldn't tell him until she had a cheque in hand.

"So, how was your dinner party?" Jewel asked.

"Revealing," Rory replied, looking at her. "You should have been there."

"I know. Sorry I missed it. I can't wait for us to throw our own dinner parties like Jill and Larry. I want to release my inner chef and try cooking some exotic dishes."

Rory smiled. "And you have Jill next door. She can teach you a thing or two. She's the master of her craft. Dinner was so good."

"Oh, yes," Jewel said. "Did you carry over leftovers?"

"Of course. I have tons of leftovers. Jill did curry goat, especially for you, and she sent over half of a Black Forest cake."

"I'll have dinner for breakfast tomorrow," Jewel said happily. "But for now, I'm dead on my feet. I'm going to shower and then hit the sack."

Rory looked at her contemplatively. "Tomorrow, I'll tell you some things I learned at the dinner party."

"Like what?" Jewel frowned.

"A bizarre story about Lester and Octavia, and who might be Mercedes's potential father."

"I'm not that tired," Jewel said. "I've always been curious

about Mercedes's background. I know she's adopted. I didn't want to seem nosy and ask too many questions about it, though."

"Go and shower," Rory said. "When you get back, I'll have a bedtime story for you."

Jewel showered in record time. She loved Rory's stories. He usually told her about the plot of a movie, and he was so good at retelling that she'd feel as if she'd watched it when he was done.

"So, tell me," she said when she came out of the shower and pulled on her sleep shirt. Rory proceeded to tell her, and she interrupted him several times, especially when she heard about Octavia's actions.

"So, are you saying that Octavia took a mentally unwell woman and farmed her out to one or more of her family members or her husband's family members just so that she could have a baby because she couldn't have one for herself?"

"That's the story," Rory nodded.

"That's sick," Jewel mumbled sleepily. "No wonder your mother hates Lester, Octavia, and me because I look like Octavia. I get it now."

Rory pulled her into him and kissed the back of her neck. "Are you going to cut her some slack from now on?"

"Hell, no," Jewel said sleepily. "Bunny needs to get in her head that I am not my family, and she needs to stop thinking I am some evil stand-in for Octavia. She needs to cut me some slack and start treating me like an individual in my own right and not an extension of my family."

"I can't argue with that," Rory murmured in her hair. "Remember, I'll be out of town for three days."

"Oh, yes," Jewel turned to him. "Your first large solo project. Everything on track?"

"Oh, yes," Rory nodded. "I actually think it's too easy so far. When I go to the actual site, I'll know more."

****

Hey, Mom," Rory greeted her. "How are you? I hope you're not here to chastise me for taking a few more guys to work on my house. I want it done before Christmas. Jewel and I can go furniture shopping in the new year."

"Oh," Bunny replied. "I'm not here because of that. I actually came to apologize for my behavior over the last couple of years. Bobby and I spoke last night after I told you all about Octavia and my suspicions about Lester being Mercedes's father. I even made an appointment with a therapist as recommended, but then I got this from my private investigator, and I am honestly stumped as to what to do right now. I know you're off for a few days, but I just had to let you know about this."

"What?" Rory picked up the folder. There were loads of pictures. Jewel at Marcel Dixon's house.

Jewel and Kenny saying goodbye to him and another man in the courtyard.

They all looked chummy together.

He swallowed. "Who is the other guy?" Rory asked.

"Richard Tinsdale," Bunny said.

"He's an architect. We offered him a job a couple of years ago, but he went on his own, and he's doing property development now. He is doing pretty well for himself."

"I see," Rory put down the pictures. "When was this?"

"Last night."

"Jewel had a work thing last night. She came in late; she was happy. This was the work thing, apparently."

"What are you going to do?" Bunny asked, concerned.

"Nothing," Rory said. His hands were trembling. Why

were his hands trembling? Maybe because he was facing one of his biggest fears. The fear that Jewel was cheating on him.

"I'll ask her to leave," Bunny said passionately. "I'll have her pack her things and go." Rory looked at his mother, feeling numb.

"No, you're going to stay out of this. This is between me and Jewel."

"She's obviously cheating on you. It was only a matter of time before this would happen," Bunny said.

"She is not cheating on me," Rory said weakly.

Jewel didn't act like a woman who was dissatisfied with him. But why was she so unhappy the other day? And then suddenly, last night, she seemed different. Happier. Lighter.

"Marcel is a known heartbreaker. Richard is an older, more established man…" Bunny hammered his insecurities with her words.

"And I trust Jewel," Rory said through gritted teeth. "I'm not jumping to conclusions and I'm not giving in to paranoia.

"If you don't stop this, I'm leaving here. I'm cutting ties with this business. I'm going to build my house elsewhere. I'm sick and tired of this!"

He had raised his voice at his mother.

It was unheard of.

Bunny widened her eyes in consternation. "You're angry at the wrong person, Rory. She got up. "I am not going to stand by while you throw away your life with this woman."

Chapter Twenty

"We need to talk. Meet me at my office at 1." Jewel read the text from her uncle as soon as it came in.

She wasn't feeling so hot. Her head ached, her throat felt itchy, and the AC in the office felt like it was stifling her. It was a little after twelve, and the day seemed as if it was slowly crawling along.

She was seriously thinking of taking the rest of the day. She felt like curling up into a ball in her bed and closing her eyes. Maybe it was a good thing that Rory wasn't going to be around to catch whatever it was she was coming down with.

She would meet her uncle at one and then drive home and sleep off whatever she had. There was a small hammer chipping away at the back of her eyes, and she couldn't concentrate on the screen. She got up and felt slightly dizzy.

"Hey Marcel," she looked at Marcel, who wasn't looking so well either. He had on an extra jacket over his shirt. "I'm not feeling so well. I'm going home."

"Okay," Marcel said. "I'll be leaving shortly. I think I caught a bug from my niece."

"So, it's not just me," Susan piped in. "I've been feeling weird since yesterday."

"It seems as if I made you all sick," Marcel said regretfully. "It's okay to go home too, Susan. The rest of the team didn't come in today because they weren't feeling well either. We'll work from home until everyone is better."

Jewel frowned. "I should call Kenny and see if she's okay. We were all at your house yesterday."

"I am sorry," Marcel said. "I deeply apologize."

"There should be a way to sue you for making us ill," Susan grumbled.

Jewel grabbed her bag. "I am just going to get some natural juice from the juice place, pop in and visit my uncle as requested, and then sleep out the rest of the day. Luckily, my husband is not around to catch this bug from me."

"He probably caught it already," Marcel said. "Let's hope not, though."

Jewel nodded. "Gotta go. I have to meet with my uncle while I am strong enough."

On the fifteen-minute drive to Leonard's office, she began to overthink things. Why did he want a meeting with me? she wondered. What were the odds that he wanted to talk just when she was seeing her way through to pay him back?

What was he planning? Was he going to move up the deadline? Was he going to quiz me about Pearl's whereabouts?

She was one month out from his impossible deadline of full payback. She dearly wished he wasn't messing with the timeline again.

She was this close to finalizing her app sale and having

some breathing room. She started formulating her arguments in case he had moved up the timeline.

She would point out to him that she had funds on the way and would pay him back in full as soon as she got the money in her account.

His offices were next to a pharmacy, a doctor, and a natural juice place. The way her throat was feeling, maybe she needed to visit all three when she was done.

When she walked into the building, the receptionist smiled at her. "You are early. Luckily, Mr. Crooks is free right now. You can go on in."

Jewel nodded.

When she walked into Leonard's office, he was surprisingly pleasant. "Jewel, have a seat."

"Thank you," Jewel said. "Full disclosure, I am not feeling well. I am trying to stay a few feet from you."

"Ah," he looked at her. "Your eyes look a bit watery. It must be that bug that's going around. A few of my employees have it. It doesn't last long. Some water, rest, and you should be fine."

Jewel nodded. "I figure that is what the doctor will say, too, if I end up going."

"Mmmph," Leonard crossed his arms in front of him and glared at her. "I wanted to meet because I wanted to know why you had to tell the Nelsons our business? The arrangement for your schooling is between Pearl and me. I only shortened the deadline for you to pay me back to get Pearl to stay. As for the threats of making you my mistress, it was purely to make her angry enough not to leave."

"I figured that out," Jewel said huskily, "but I didn't tell the Nelsons anything. I may have mentioned to my husband that I owe you for my schooling, but as far as he is concerned, I have two years to pay you back. He offered to pay you back himself, and I told him I would do it. I am selling an app. The sales haven't been finalized yet, though. I may just be able to make it for the deadline."

"Don't bother," Leonard said gruffly. "Your mother-in-law paid back your loan today, an hour ago."

"Say what?" Jewel widened her eyes. Her headache had temporarily vanished. "Bunny Nelson paid you back?"

"Yes, and she had the gall to threaten me to leave you alone. What have you been telling her about me?"

"Nothing," Jewel was really confused. "I didn't even know that she knew...am I dreaming this?"

"No, you are not," Leonard huffed. "Now my main bargaining chip to get Pearl back is gone, and I can't even bring her back by force. She's moving in circles. I'm afraid to breach. She has aligned herself with some powerful people."

"Which people?" Jewel asked, confused.

"Pearl won't tell you details because she knows I will ask," Leonard said. "She is smart. Next time you talk to her, tell her I am begging her to come back, okay?"

"She won't do that," Jewel said.

"I know," Leonard nodded. "Tell her I will not stop until she is back. I don't care who is on her side. I invested too much in Pearl Day for her to slip away."

Jewel stood up and held on to the desk to steady herself. "Well, Uncle Leonard, that's between you and my mother. I am going to have a lie-down."

"You do that," Leonard said dismissively.

"And thank you for helping when you did."

He waved her off. "It was nothing."

****

Jewel stopped by the natural juice store. Her mother swore by these people's juices for all sorts of ailments. Her tiny headache had turned into a full-fledged pounding.

"I have a headache, and I am coming down with something," she said to the guy at the counter.

"Okay," he nodded. "I am going to give you something for the headache now and a couple of liters of flu juice."

"Flu juice?" Jewel chuckled weakly.

"Yep," he said as he started busying himself around the counter. She saw him grab ginger, and she sat down and waited for him to blend it with the other ingredients. He served it to her in a glass with a straw.

"Sit tight. I am going to give you a liter of fresh juice to bolster your immune system."

She slowly sipped the juice, which was good. It had lemon, ginger, carrot, and some berries, she didn't know exactly what was in it, but her headache started to slowly recede the more she drank. When she left with her juices, she was feeling a little better and thinking more clearly about the good news that Leonard had just dropped on her.

After a nap, she would thank Bunny profusely for paying her school fees. It was totally unexpected and heartwarming for her to fork out millions of dollars to pay for her. Out of her two in-laws, she would have expected Bobby to do it if he ever found out that she had the debt, but not Bunny. Never, Bunny. What could be her motivation?

Was it the fact that she had finally made it known why she didn't like her because she resembled Octavia? What could it be? When she drove up to the yard and parked in front of the driveway, she saw that Bunny's vehicle was parked outside too, which meant she was home early, which was rare.

Jewel got out of the car. The refreshed feeling after the

juice was wearing off, and she really needed a nap. Maybe if she had hurried toward her door, she wouldn't have run into Bunny now. She didn't want a one-on-one with Bunny just yet, as she took lots of energy to deal with. Her hopes for a quick escape were dashed when the door from the garage opened and Bunny appeared.

"I saw you drive up. It's quite early for you to be home, isn't it?" Bunny said.

Jewel nodded. "Everyone on my team is sick. Seems as if we caught a bug from Marcel." She added, "I heard you paid back my loan to my uncle. I would have thanked you later after I rested for a while."

"It was nothing to pay back your loan, Jewel," Bunny replied. "If I had known you had that burden on your head, I would have done it long ago."

Jewel was floored. She had no idea Bunny would be so generous and kind. "Thank you," she stammered. "I wanted to pay him off myself, but he moved up the deadline after my mother left."

"I know how he treats his ex-mistresses," Bunny said. "I know everything about you, your past and even your current situation."

"You do?" Jewel asked.

"Yes," Bunny nodded. "Do you know why I paid back your school fee?"

Jewel shook her head. "I am still trying to figure that out."

"Because I wanted you to owe me," Bunny said. "I wanted you to do exactly as I asked without argument."

Jewel looked at her mother-in-law, dread holding her in place. What would this woman, who hated her, ask her to do?

She didn't have long to wait.

"I want you to leave, Rory. I want you to pack your bags

today and go."

"You can't be serious," Jewel said weakly.

"But I am," Bunny said. "There's no reason for you to stay and torture my son. You have other relationships. I told him about them. I showed him the evidence. Knowing him, he will try and make it work with you. It's up to me to ensure he doesn't get his heart broken."

"I don't have other relationships," Jewel gasped.

"What about Richard Tinsdale or Marcel Dixon?" Bunny exclaimed. "See, you even got a bug from him."

"Those are not romantic relationships," Jewel said. "It's strictly business."

"Good Lord, you admit that to me?" Bunny exclaimed. "Don't you have any shame?"

"What's the big deal in admitting it to you?" Jewel was confused. Her headache had started up again, along with her stress levels. "Richard needed what I have to offer, and in return, I will get paid. In a couple of months, I wouldn't have needed you to pay my uncle at all. I would have done that myself."

"You are married!" Bunny shouted. "Doesn't Rory mean anything to you?"

"Of course he does," Jewel held her head. "I didn't want to involve him in this because it is my debt. And frankly, I was scared you'd call me a gold digger. You have been implying that I am one for a while now."

"You know what? Pack your bags and go," Bunny snarled. "Leave my house. You're worse than a gold digger. I have never met anyone like you."

Jewel inhaled deeply. She didn't know why Bunny had this reaction to her having a business relationship with Richard Tinsdale, and she was too sick to decipher it now. The woman looked like she wanted to strangle her, and to be frank, if she attempted to, Jewel couldn't put up much of a fight.

"I'll call Rory and tell him about this," Jewel mumbled. "I can't just leave without telling him why."

"No, you won't tell him," Bunny said. "When I said you are not to tell Rory anything about this... That boy loves you past all reasoning. He'll probably accept this and make excuses for you. If you tell him, I am taking that money back from your uncle."

Jewel sighed. "I can't just leave my husband, Bunny. I love him. You can't bribe me to leave. I'll pay you or my uncle back soon enough. I am too sick to argue with you, so I am going away until Rory returns. Whatever your issues are, you need to sort them out and soon. You are acting like a lunatic."

"Argh," Bunny headed toward her.

Jewel actually held her hand up to shield her face from a slap. When it didn't come, she opened her eyes and saw Mercedes holding her mother back.

"Mom, go inside and let me handle this," Mercedes said firmly to Bunny.

"Did you hear what she said to me?" Bunny asked.

"I did," Mercedes nodded. "I'll deal with this."

Bunny glared at her and shrugged her arm out of Mercedes' grip. "I am going back to work; you better not be here when I get home."

Jewel nodded.

"You, okay?" Mercedes asked when Bunny drove out of the yard, tires squealing.

"No, actually," Jewel said weakly, "I am not feeling well and was almost assaulted by Bunny. It's a good thing that you were here."

"She really was acting like a lunatic," Mercedes said. "You

were right. In all my years of living with Bonita Nelson, I have never seen her so angry. I wonder what brought that on."

"I don't know," Jewel said. "I'll try to tell you on my way to someplace else other than here. I am feeling so out of sorts though, I have no idea if I can drive."

"I'll drive you," Mercedes said, "unless you want to stay with me."

"No, I think some time away from here and near Bunny is on the cards," Jewel said. "I honestly don't feel like sleeping with one eye open. I should go pack a bag."

"I'll help you," Mercedes said. "I'll get my car and drive you to wherever you want. I'll also call Rory and tell him where you are so he doesn't have to worry."

"You are really the coolest sister," Jewel said, leaning on the car. Her skin was feeling prickly and sensitive. Maybe she had a fever. What a day it was turning out to be.

Chapter Twenty-One

Rory sat on the patio at his aunt's luxurious house and watched the sunset. He wished Jewel was around. She would love the explosion of colors in the sky.

But she wasn't answering her phone. He called her for what felt like the hundredth time, and then he started to fret. He should have called her this morning as soon as he found out that his mother had taken pictures of her at Marcel's house and clarified with her why she had gone there with Kenny.

There had to be an explanation for that. Maybe he was too confident, but he didn't buy the assertations his mother was making against her. If she was cheating on him with Marcel, why bring Kenny?

Besides, Jewel loved him. He felt her love. He had no reason to second-guess her genuine feelings for him or suspect her of cheating. He was getting desperate, though, to hear from her.

He called Kenny, and she wasn't answering her phone either. Maybe they had a work thing. Maybe they were back at Marcel's place, a little voice whispered in his head.

Maybe Kenny was paired up with Marcel and Richard with Jewel.

He refused to entertain that thought. He shut it down immediately.

He called his mother to find out if Jewel was at home.

"I am still at the office, dear," Bunny said chirpily. "Not getting through to Jewel?"

"No," Rory sighed.

"Well then, maybe you should check her boyfriend?" Bunny said, trying to sound helpful. "It's quite likely that she went straight to him since you're away. I have to go, dear. It's still busy over here."

Before he could protest her calling Marcel, Jewel's boyfriend, she hung up the phone.

Several calls later, with no answer from Jewel's phone, Rory called Shay to ask for Marcel's number. Shay gave it to him, and Rory stared at the number and the phone, part of him reluctant to dial it, another part of him wanting to know.

If Jewel was really cheating on him with Marcel, what would he do? He had no clue. He knew it would break him, and he didn't know if he would ever recover.

His mother's casual mention of his wife cheating was cruel and indicative of the fact that she had no idea how much it hurt to hear her say such a thing outright.

Rory ran his hand over his face. He had a fearful feeling in the pit of his stomach. None of this made sense.

Jewel had been fine when he left her that morning. He refused to believe she was cheating or had left him, and that belief gave him the confidence he needed to dial the number in front of him. Marcel answered the phone after several rings.

"Whoever this is, I am dying," Marcel answered.

Rory cleared his throat. "You are?"

"Yup," Marcel said hoarsely. "The flu medication is not working. Who is this?"

"Rory Nelson, I was wondering, have you seen Jewel?"

"Not since she left early today," Marcel murmured. "The whole team got sick. If she feels half of what I feel, I think she's probably knocked out and in bed, trying to sleep off this bug."

"Thank you," Rory said in relief.

Marcel hung up. And Rory dialed Jill's number. Jill was the best at taking care of sick people.

"Jill, could you check on Jewel for me?" Rory asked. "I just heard that she's sick and not answering her phone."

"I suspect that's why Mercedes took her to Cascade Hills," Jill said. "I begged them to stay at my apartment above the bakery, but Jewel insisted that she needed to be around her family. Apparently, she and your mother got into it again."

Rory groaned.

"Don't worry, Mercedes is with her," Jill said. "I suspect you haven't heard from her because the reception is sketchy up there."

****

Jewel settled into her grandmother's guest room. She wanted to talk to Rory, but Mercedes had reassured her that she would take care of everything. Her grandmother had accepted her showing up without much fanfare. She constantly checked on her and fed her the flu juice and water. It was one day down, even though Jewel felt as if she was sleeping forever.

Her father stopped by.

"Why are you up here?" Darnell said. "Where's your hubby?"

"He's away on a job," Jewel said weakly, "and I had a fight with his mother."

"Ah, the Nelsons don't strike me as the family feud kind of people," Darnell felt her forehead. "You're burning up."

"Grandma said the fever was coming down. She takes my temperature regularly," Jewel cleared her throat. "What are you doing up here? I thought you lived with your girlfriend in the town."

"Relationship problems," Darnell shrugged. "Sometimes I come up here for a breather, and it's the weekend. Nobody wants a nagging woman in their ears on the weekend."

"Look at the both of us," Jewel chuckled. "Taking refuge back home when we have nowhere else to go, Grandpa Reese would be proud."

"He wouldn't be proud of me, but he would be proud of you," Darnell stretched out beside her. "You married a nice boy from a good family, graduated college, and have a steady, nice job in one of those fancy business places. You ticked all the boxes with no help from me. I have to lift my hat off to Pearl. She did a good job with you."

"I'm going to make sure I tell her that the next time I talk to her," Jewel smiled.

"I saw her at your graduation party," Darnell smiled. "She looks good, gorgeous, even like life is treating her right. If I had a dollar for how often I have thought about going back to Pearl and making a life with her, I would be rich."

"She would never in a million years take you back," Jewel laughed.

"I wouldn't say never," Darnell laughed. "She could have amnesia and all her memories of me are wiped. And if she hadn't met my oldest brother, David, we could make a go of it again."

"I'd tell her not to do it," Jewel murmured. "And what do you mean 'if she hadn't met Uncle David'? He's not rich."

"Pearl has always put certain people, in a certain income bracket, on a pedestal," Darnell sighed. "She met David after he came back from the farm worker program. Back in those days, I guess David seemed like he was rich and made of money. He dressed in the latest fashions, bought a car, and flashed his cash around. The both of us were still in high school. A high school boy has no cash to flash.

"Anyway, Pearl had a crush on David that was so severe, I was jealous as hell. She would talk about him daily: David is cute, David is rich, and I could see myself with David."

Darnell imitated Pearl's voice so accurately that it had Jewel giggling.

"And I heard she was getting a lift in David's car a few times." Darnell continued, "When she got pregnant, I was so jealous, I was convinced the child was David's.

"I've never heard that story," Jewel said.

"Because it doesn't show her in a good light?" Darnell said. "And I haven't told you the half of it. Needless to say, David swears to this day that he never touched her. It didn't matter at the time, and it hardly matters now. Her infatuation with him was a turn-off and affected the relationship I could have had with you, my firstborn."

"I thought I had truly loved Pearl at the time, but who knows how long we would have lasted even without David in the picture. Pearl and I are so different, like chalk and cheese. And we were so young and immature. But, to be honest, I think I am still a little immature."

Jewel smiled. "Now admitting that takes maturity."

"It is going to take maturity to get over whatever problems

you have with Bunny," Darnell said. "Even though people are older than you age-wise, sometimes you will have to be the more mature one in the relationship."

Jewel opened her eyes and blinked at Darnell. "You don't even know what the problem is."

"It doesn't matter," Darnell replied. "Take a mature approach to this, and the problem will be solved." Darnell looked at his watch. "I should leave you to get some rest."

"Night," Jewel said sleepily.

"Goodnight, baby girl," Darnell said as he left.

Long after he left, Jewel pondered how she should take a mature approach to Bunny's obvious dislike. The thoughts followed her into her dream, and she had one loopy scenario after another playing out in her head. She woke up in the middle of the night shivering and with a headache. She felt the sheet lifting, and a warm body curved along hers.

"Rory," she murmured.

"Yes," he whispered.

"Am I dreaming?" Jewel asked.

"Nope," Rory replied. "I had to wrap up my visit to St. Mary this evening. I couldn't stay away one day more after I heard you weren't well."

Jewel inhaled deeply. "I love you."

"I love you more," Rory whispered. "In sickness and in health.

"Till death do us part." Jewel snuggled into him, feeling warm and safe.

Chapter Twenty-Two

Jewel was still feeling weak, but Rory insisted they needed to go home.

"Mercedes convened a family meeting," Rory said. "She's calling it an intervention. Sadly, I think my mother needs it, and we all need to get everything out in the clear. You don't have to stay for the whole thing, but if we don't do this, I don't think I can continue living or working with my mother. What she did to you a few days ago, ordering you to leave like that, was unconscionable. She needs to understand that you are my family now, and I am choosing you. I'll always choose you."

Jewel smiled. "Even though she showed you irrefutable proof of my so-called cheating?"

"Even then," Rory said. "For a couple of minutes, I wavered and almost had a nervous breakdown when I thought of you with someone else, but I remembered who you are. You love me. I can feel it."

"I do love you," Jewel said. "And I can feel your love too."

"I wish we had talked about you selling an app to Richard Tinsdale to pay back your uncle, though. I didn't know he had moved up the deadline. I could have easily paid it off with the inheritance I will receive on my twenty-first birthday next week."

Jewel smiled. "So you are a rich guy next week? How is it that I am just hearing about this?"

"Because I liked that you were with me for me," Rory shrugged. "I didn't want money to come between us."

"Mmm," Jewel said. "I think I liked when we were on equal footing."

"But we wouldn't be," Rory grinned. "Next week, you will be the rich girl when you make millions from your app. In a way, we are now on equal footing. And now that you realize that you can sell apps for millions, I have no doubt you will be out-earning me in no time. Please note that I loved you before you were a rich girl."

Jewel laughed. "Noted."

****

"I am so sorry I am dragging you through this when you are still sick, Jewel," Mercedes greeted them at the entrance to her living room. It was Jewel's first time in Mercedes' house; she had only recently spent the time to furnish and decorate the whole place. Her place was done in black and white with subtle shades of blue. It looked chic and sophisticated but homey at the same time. Jewel was impressed. "Wow," she looked around. "Larry did a good job with the décor. Look at those pictures! Is that from the gallery where you bought the O. Dennis paintings?"

"I am the decorator," Mercedes laughed. "And the pictures

were taken by me. It's a hobby. I will help you decorate when you guys are ready. I just finished decorating last month; it took me a while to find the right pieces."

"You are my first guests," Mercedes said. "We should go onto the patio. I thought we could sit out there. I arranged the chairs in a circle. Lester sent over some tapes that I think we can watch together."

"Lester Webb?" Rory and Jewel asked almost at the same time.

"One and the same," Mercedes said. "I had a long chat with him yesterday. I called him to ask him if he is my father."

"Is he?" Jewel asked.

"No," Mercedes shook her head. "And once again, I think Mom got it all wrong with Octavia and Claudia and all of it. Let's wait for the others to get here, and then we'll all begin to clear up years of misunderstandings."

Larry and Jill came soon after. Jill brought refreshments, cakes, scones, and little curried goat patties. "I wish I could taste it," Jewel muttered. "I love those curried goat patties."

Jill patted her hand. "Don't you worry. I can throw a party for you when you get better."

Jeremiah and Shay arrived without the children.

"My mom is watching them," Shay said when asked where they were. They chit-chatted for a bit. Mercedes called Bobby, who apologized for running late. He had to convince Bunny that they weren't about to gang up on her. Half an hour later, Bobby and Bunny arrived.

Bunny paused when she saw them sitting together in a circle. She glared at each of them one by one and gasped when she saw Jewel. That's when she hugged her husband's hand for dear life. When they both sat down, Mercedes said, "Thank you all for coming. I have staged a fair amount of family interventions in my capacity as a therapist, and I shouldn't be nervous about this, but you are my family, and this hits close to home.

"A few days ago, my mother assumed the wrong thing, and it caused some friction between her and Jewel, her daughter-in-law. I would like to clear that up now before we proceed. Jewel, could you kindly explain to Bunny why you were meeting with Richard Tinsdale and Marcel Dixon at his home?"

Jewel inhaled, "Richard is interested in an app that Kenny and I built. Marcel brokered the arrangement, that's why we met at his house. I told Bunny that it was a professional business arrangement. I don't know what she assumed. I can only imagine that it wasn't complimentary to me or Kenny. She was so mad; I think she was heading toward me to slap my face."

"I was," Bunny said, removing her glasses. "I thought you were casually talking about sleeping with other people while married to my son. I defend my own. But you were selling an app?"

"He is paying her twenty million for it," Rory said.

"Oh, my," Bunny opened her mouth. "I did jump to conclusions. I am very sorry, Jewel."

"Why don't we have this app?" Bobby asked. "Aren't we in property development too? Why aren't you designing one for us?"

Jewel chuckled. "I initially designed it with your company in mind. I had a lot of input from Jeremiah. He said you liked doing things old school, and you probably wouldn't be interested."

"Well, if Richard Tinsdale is paying twenty million dollars for it, I am interested in it," Bobby said.

Everybody chuckled.

Mercedes nodded. "Good, we are off to a great start. Mom, you tried to bribe Jewel off the premises?"

"I did," Bunny nodded. "My PI found out that her uncle was the one who paid her school fees, and he was using it to get her mother to come back to work for him. So, I paid the debt, and then I told Jewel that she owed me and needed to leave Rory."

"Goodness," Larry whistled. "I didn't know people did these things in real life. That's soap opera-level stuff."

Bunny inhaled. "I was wrong."

"I'll be repaying you in full for that," Jewel said. "As soon as I can."

"There is no need to," Bunny said. "I never meant to hold it over your head."

"I will pay you back, though," Jewel said. "I like paying my debts, and I don't want to be beholden to you. It's a matter of pride. I never wanted Rory to do it, and I don't want you to either."

"Okay, that's fine," Mercedes turned to Bunny. "There is no need to argue."

Bunny sighed. "I am not going to. It seems as if I misjudged you severely, Jewel."

"Which brings us to why you instantly disliked Jewel," Mercedes said. "It stems from her resemblance to Octavia, who you said captured Claudia to have the babies she couldn't."

Bunny nodded. "Those assumptions are unfounded," Mercedes sighed. "I had a long conversation with Lester, and he sent me copies of some tapes he found with Octavia and Claudia. By the way, he is not my father. He had a vasectomy done after his affair with you, Mom."

"Lester also said Octavia was so protective of Claudia that her pregnancy was a surprise. Claudia wouldn't tell her who my father was, and Octavia became paranoid that it was her ex-husband. She wasn't pleased to find that out at all. Lester theorizes that they were arguing about it when they met in that accident."

"Without further ado, let us watch this clip."

It was a beach background, and two smiling faces came on camera. Octavia Webb looked a lot like her, Jewel had to admit, and Claudia looked fresh and pretty.

"Today is Claudia's twenty-second birthday! Yay," Octavia kissed her cheeks. "I met this young lady a year ago while visiting Cascade Hills. When I was down and out and going through a dreadful experience in my life, I saw her at the side of the road with her thumb sticking out. She wanted a drive. She wanted to escape. Escape what? I asked."

"Boredom, my life here. They all treat me like a child," Octavia sighed. "I couldn't just take her away. I told her to get in the car, then I doubled back to where she said she had lived. I told her parents that I would take her for a while. Her parents protested but were happy that I wasn't some axe murderer. That was the eighth time that month that Claudia had attempted to run away."

"It was more than that," Claudia said in a child-like voice. "I left, but I always went back. I had nowhere to go. Everybody treated me like a child with no sense."

"So I took her in," Octavia said. "We had a great year. God sent her because he knew that I needed to heal. I think of Claudia as my angel. I love her. Maybe she is the daughter that I will never have."

"And yesterday, we learned from her therapist that with long-term treatment, she can be relatively normal," Octavia continued. "Her birth trauma caused some serious developmental delays. All Claudia needed was someone to help and take her seriously. I am her family now."

Bunny started sobbing and headed for the guest room. There wasn't a dry eye in the group. Even Mercedes was blinking rapidly.

"Pause that," Bobby said, taking out his handkerchief and wiping his eye. "I have to go and see my wife. I think she got a lot of things wrong, and she will need some time."

Mercedes nodded. They watched as Bobby went after Bunny. Jewel was too choked up to speak.

"Thank you, Mercedes, for sorting that out," Jewel finally managed to say. "It must be devastating for Bunny to find out that the story that has been in her head for years is so wrong."

"And if she was wrong about this, maybe she was wrong about Lester trying to kill her," Jeremiah said. "I have always thought of him as the enemy."

"Or maybe we can throw another intervention with him as a special guest," Rory said. "I am thankful for this. I see this as the beginning of healing and letting old assumptions rest. I have to get Jewel to bed."

"I also think it will be a new era of Jewel and Bunny having a better relationship," Mercedes said. "And that's what tonight was about."

Jewel walked over and hugged Mercedes. "I know seeing that cannot have been easy. If you need to talk, I am here."

"Thank you," Mercedes said.

"Do you think Bunny will be okay?" Jewel asked when they were out of earshot.

"Of course," Rory said. "She will come around. She will kill you with apologies. It will take time, but I am sure that you two will eventually have a cordial relationship or even more. Who knows?"

"From your mouth to God's ears," Jewel said jokingly.

Epilogue

Jewel and Rory's Housewarming Party

The house wasn't ready for Christmas or even January, but it was finished and furnished for Valentine's Day, and they decided to throw a party. The backyard house was perfect for entertaining. They had pitched a tent, decorated the place in red, and were throwing a Valentine's-themed party. Most of Jewel's closest family members were there, except for Pearl, who was still lying low.

Her father, cousin Lester, grandmother, and grandaunt were sitting at one table. It was quite a sight to see Lester Webb and Bonita Nelson in the same space. They had even greeted each other politely. There was a truce of sorts afoot. Bunny acknowledged publicly that she had misjudged the Webb family, painting them all with the same misguided hatred that she had for Lester and Octavia. She was seeing a therapist to talk it through.

Her relationship with Jewel had taken a turn for the

better. They had even shopped for furniture together, and as a bonding activity, it had been successful. They both appreciated the positives in each other's personalities. To the family's relief, there were no more barbs traded between the two women when Jewel joined them for dinner.

They were sitting at the head table, and their MC, for the moment, was Camden. "It's toast time," Camden tapped his glass. "And I am going first. To Rory and Jewel."

He raised his glass, and everyone chuckled. "To Rory and Jewel."

"See, that was short and sweet," Camden said. "Who is next?"

"I am," Rory stood up. "Three years ago, I proposed to Jewel, and she said yes. It feels like just yesterday. I love her more and more each day. She brings light into my life and makes every day brighter. So, let us raise a glass to the love of my life, Jewel. Here's to many more years of happiness and love. Cheers!"

"I am next," Jewel stood up. "Rory, we just built a house, a place to call our own. I remember Kenny making a speech at our wedding and saying that we should consider each other home, not the mortar and block edifice that we have here but each other. I said it three years ago, and I mean it now, Rory. I am happy we have our own house, but you are home at the end of the day; there is no place like you! Cheers!"

The room erupted in applause and cheers. Jewel felt a sense of peace wash over her as they clinked their glasses together.

"No place like you, Jewel," Rory said before sealing the vow with a kiss.

The End

Want to know more about Pearl and her escape from Leonard? Check out:

Knight and Day

Pearl Day had finally broken free from Leonard's grip as the manager of Sensuous City, but little did she know that her heart would become entangled with the charming gardener, Phil Knight, at her new job.

Despite her unhappy past with men, Pearl was ready to take a chance on love, but could she let go of her high standards and embrace a man who wasn't wealthy?

And even if she did, would she survive the wrath of Leonard, who was determined to track her down and exact his revenge on her for leaving?

No Expectations (Crimson Hill Book 9)

Mercedes finds herself captivated by a striking photograph of Dr. Charles Payne, displayed in a brochure for a health retreat. Yet, it isn't just his handsome appearance that piques her interest. A baffling mystery surrounds Charles—an uncanny resemblance to both the Wessons of Crimson Hills and Maud Beecher's long-lost baby. Driven by curiosity and a desire for answers, Mercedes embarks on a quest to uncover the truth behind this perplexing connection. With each revelation, the bond between Mercedes and Charles strengthens, and they find themselves irresistibly drawn to one another.

For Charles, meeting Mercedes face to face at the health retreat is a surreal experience. She had always been his dream girl, and now fate has brought them together in the most unexpected of circumstances. However, his joy is tempered by the haunting possibility that Mercedes may be linked to the Monroes—a family he had vowed to forget and leave behind forever.

As their paths intertwine, Mercedes and Charles embark on a journey of self-discovery, unearthing long-buried secrets that could either bring them closer or tear them apart.

Discover Exclusive Offers and Be the First to Know!

If you haven't already, don't miss out on the opportunity to join my New Release Newsletter! Sign up today and become part of an exclusive community where you'll be among the first to hear about my latest book releases and take advantage of special prices.

Why join my mailing list?

Be the First: Get a head start and be the first to know when I release a new book.

Exclusive Discounts: Unlock special prices available only to subscribers. Enjoy limited time offers and save big on your favorite books.

Quick and Easy: Signing up takes less than 30 seconds.

To join, visit https://www.brenalbar.com/newsletter or scan the QR code below.

Thank you for your support, and happy reading!

The Crimson Hill Series

Where family drama, romance, and a touch of sci-fi blend seamlessly in the enchanting backdrop of a small town in Jamaica. Prepare to embark on an unforgettable journey as secrets unravel, passions ignite, and destinies intertwine.

No Goodbye (Book 1)
No Misunderstanding (Book 2)
No Ordinary Love (Book 3)
No Fairy Tale (Book 4)
No Letting Go (Book 5)
No Strings Attached (Book 6)
No More Mrs. Nice Girl (Book 7)
No Place Like You (Book 8)
Knight and Day (Book 8.5)
No Expectations (Book 9)
Ice and Fyre (Book 9.5)
No Surrender (Book 10)
No Time for Love (Book 11)
No Promises (Book 12)
Winter's Eve (Book 13)

The Wiley Brothers

Step into the world of the Wiley Brothers, where tragedy weaves an unbreakable bond and love becomes their guiding light. In this captivating series, follow the journey of six remarkable boys as they navigate the tumultuous path of growing up without parents, discovering love, and finding their place in a challenging world.

Between Brothers (Book 0)- How it all began…
For Pete's Sake (Book 1)- Preston's story.
Crossing Jordan (Book 2)-Jordan's story.
Fire and Walter (Book 3)- Walter's story.
The Perfect Guy (Book 4)-Guy's Story.
The Patience of a Saint (Book 5)- Saint's Story.
A Case of Love (Book 6)- Case's Story.

The Pryce Sisters

Follow the remarkable journey of the Pryce triplets as they navigate the complexities of growing up, discovering romance, and embracing the exhilarating challenges of the new adult years.

Baby For A Pryce- Book 1
Right Pryce Wrong Time – Book 2
Yours, For A Pryce- Book 3

The Jacksons

Prepare to be enthralled by the captivating saga of the Jackson family. In this gripping series, secrets unravel, paternity questions loom, and love blooms in the most unexpected corners.

Ace- Book 1
Deuce- Book 2
Trey- Book 3
Quade- Book 4

The Scarlett Series

Their patriarch died and unexpectedly left each of them a fortune. Watch as the Scarlett family navigate their way through the ups and downs of sudden wealth, family secrets, and the complicated dynamics of their relationships.

Scarlett Baby (Book 1)
Scarlett Sinner (Book 2)
Scarlett Secret (Book 3)
Scarlett Love (Book 4)
Scarlett Promise (Book 5)
Scarlett Bride (Book 6)
Scarlett Heart (Book 7)

Magnolia Sisters

They were the rejects. The worst of the lot, they grew up in a girl's home together and formed sisterly bonds. Each book in the series tells the story of a different girl and the unique struggles and triumphs she faces along the way. With themes of friendship, forgiveness, and the power of love, the "Magnolia Sisters" series is a heartwarming and inspiring read that you won't want to put down.

Dear Mystery Guy- Book 1
Bad Girl Blues- Book 2
Her Mistaken Dream- Book 3
Just Like Yesterday – Book 4

New Song Series

A group of friends started out as a church band, see how each of them navigate their personal and professional lives while staying true to their faith and facing challenges along the way. With themes of forgiveness, redemption, and second chances, the New Song Series is a captivating read for anyone who enjoys heartwarming stories of love and faith.

Going Solo- Book 1
Duet on Fire- Book 2
Tangled Chords- Book 3
Broken Harmony- Book 4
A Past Refrain- Book 5
Perfect Melody- Book 6

The Bancrofts

The Bancroft family delves into the inner workings of academia and the high-stakes world of university politics. The family wrestles with the pressures of maintaining their family's legacy, they must confront their own demons and navigate the complex relationships that bind them together. From unexpected love affairs and betrayals to scandals and secrets that threaten to tear them apart, this is a series that will keep you captivated until the very end.

Homely Girl- Book 0
Saving Face- Book 1
Tattered Tiara- Book 2
Private Dancer- Book 3
Goodbye Lonely- Book 4
Practice Run- Book 5
Sense of Rumor- Book 6
A Younger Man- Book 7
Just To See Her- Book 8

Three Rivers Series

Three Rivers Series, a captivating tale of love, redemption, and second chances set in a picturesque community in St. Ann's Bay, Jamaica.

Private Sins- Book 1
Loving Mr. Wright- Book 2
Unholy Matrimony- Book 3
If It Ain't Broke- Book 4

The Resetter Series

The Resetter Series takes a look at a rare kind of person, a person who can travel back in time, but they only have one chance to get things right if they go back! With themes of second chances, changing the past and the power of love, the resetters series is a captivating time travel romance that many readers have described as a page turner.

Never Too Late- Book 1
Never Say Never- Book 2
Now or Never- Book 3
Almost Never- Book 4

On the Rebound Series

Experience the gripping and emotionally charged On the Rebound series, where love, betrayal, and redemption collide in a whirlwind of passion and secrets. Brace yourself for a journey filled with drama, cheating scandals, DNA questions, and ultimately, the power of second chances and finding love again.

On the Rebound- Book 1
On the Rebound Book 2

Standalone Books

Full Circle- After graduating from university, Diana wanted to return to Jamaica to find her siblings. What she didn't foresee was that she would meet Robert Cassidy and that both their pasts would be intertwined, and that disturbing questions would pop up about their parentage just when they were getting close.

After the End- Torn between two lovers. Colleen married her high school sweetheart, Isaiah, hoping that they would live happily ever after, but life intruded, and Isaiah disappeared at sea. She found work with the rich and handsome Enrique Lopez as a housekeeper and realized that she couldn't keep him at arm's length.

Love Triangle: Three Sides to the Story- George, the husband. Marie, the wife, and Karen-the mistress. They all get to tell their side of the story.

New Beginnings- Inner-city girl Geneva was offered an opportunity of a lifetime when she learned that her 'real' father was a wealthy man. Her decision to live up-town meant she had to leave Froggie, her 'ghetto don,' behind. She also found herself battling with her stepmother and battling her emotions for Justin, a suave up-towner.

The Preacher and the Prostitute- Prostitution and the clergy don't mix. Tell that to ex-prostitute Maribel, who finds herself in love with the Pastor at her church. Can an ex-prostitute and a pastor have a future together?

Historical Fiction

You won't want to miss out on these two captivating reads!

"The Pull of Freedom" tells the story of a slave family and their desperate struggle for freedom in Jamaica's colonial era. Follow the journey of these brave individuals as they fight for their right to be free, facing danger, heartbreak, and unimaginable obstacles along the way.

"The Empty Hammock" takes readers on a journey through time, as a modern woman finds herself transported back to the Taino era of Jamaica's history. Experience the wonder and mystery of this ancient culture through her eyes, as she learns about their traditions, beliefs, and way of life. With richly drawn characters and a beautifully realized setting, "The Empty Hammock" is a must-read for anyone who loves historical fiction that transports them to another time and place.

Short Story Collections

Di Taxi Ride and Other Stories- Funny stories about Jamaican life to make you laugh.

Book Bundles

Jamaican Romance Bundle- New Beginnings, Full Circle, Love Triangle: Three Sides to The Story, After The End

Wiley Brothers Book 0-3
Wiley Brothers Book 4-6